D0425821

Cut to:
MURDER

A HENRY HOLT MYSTERY

ALSO BY DENISE OSBORNE

Murder Offscreen

A HENRY HOLT MYSTERY

Cut to: MURDER

DENISE OSBORNE

HENRY HOLT AND COMPANY NEW YORK

Henry Holt and Company, Inc.
Publishers since 1866
115 West 18th Street
New York, New York 10011

Henry Holt® is a registered
trademark of Henry Holt and Company, Inc.

Published in Canada by Fitzhenry & Whiteside Ltd.,
195 Allstate Parkway, Markham, Ontario L3R 4T8.

Library of Congress Cataloging-in-Publication Data
Osborne, Denise.
Cut to: murder/Denise Osborne.—1st ed.
p.   cm.—(Henry Holt mystery)
I. Title.
PS3565.S374C87   1995   94-45808
813'.54—dc20   CIP

ISBN 0-8050-3114-6

Henry Holt books are available for special
promotions and premiums. For details contact:
Director, Special Markets.

First Edition—1995

DESIGNED BY PAULA R. SZAFRANSKI

Printed in the United States of America
All first editions are printed on acid-free paper.∞

1   3   5   7   9   10   8   6   4   2

To Christopher James Osborne,
my bulwark for many journeys.

Sabe esperar—
aguarda que la marea fluya
asi en la costa un barco
sin que el partir te inquieta.

—Antonio Machada

(Know how to hope—
await the rising tide
like a boat ashore
and do not fear for the departure.)

ACKNOWLEDGMENTS

THE AUTHOR WISHES to acknowledge friends and colleagues at I.E.S.E. in Barcelona, especially Miguel Lustau, Elizabeth McCormick, Richard Jones, Professor Pedro Nueno, Sara and Paul Yandell, Cristophe and Novlette Meyer, Ritta Andersson, Harri Andersson, Tim Gallagher, Dennis Heijn; Dani Bourges at the former Casa Vasca, and the always helpful and informative people at Banco Central.

For further adventures in Barcelona, Sitges, Montserrat, and Figueras, thanks go to Alberta Barker and poet Diane Barker (not only my sister, but my most delightful and brainy *sister in crime*) and, for supplemental funding, Harrison Barker.

For being so hospitable to a couple of colonials: Val and Tony Jones of Puck Hill, Surrey; Vi Daniels and Charlie, Barbara, Jimmy, David, and Ian Pomford of Ellesmere Port, Cheshire.

To those who have given generously of their resources: Dee Osborne and Jude Osborne; Dana and Mike Richmond, Signe and Carvell Nelson, Lorraine Kessler; Traci and Ava Smith; Marilyn and Mike Fitzgerald; Julie Busching Paige for the signing pen; Myra and Richard Recker for succor in San Francisco; Eddie and Jean Kessler, and Dirk Gentry. Close to home, Phil and Steve Osborne for painful puns and clever conversation.

Special thanks go to Julie Williams; to the Manhattan, Kansas Writer's Guild; and to Ben Nyberg, Steve Heller, Dean Hall, and Gary Clift in the Kansas State University English department.

Finally, books are published because of those with integrity and spirit who believe in and nurture writers—the very best being my agent, Teresa Chris, and my editor, Jo Ann Haun.

To be a film director, you really have to be a maniac—to follow the same story for five years is like every morning you take the same piece of chewing gum to see if you can still taste it.

—Jaco Van Dormael,
director, *Toto le Heros*

Barcelona, the treasure house of courtesy, the refuge of strangers ... unique in its position and its beauty. And although the adventures that befell me there occasioned me no great pleasure, but rather much grief, I bore them the better for having seen that city.

—Miguel de Cervantes,
Don Quixote, Part II

Cut to:

MURDER

A HENRY HOLT MYSTERY

February 1938
catalonia, spain

IN A MOUNTAIN village about thirty-six kilometers north-west of Gerona, Maria Raurell slipped the Luger out of a pocket in her long black skirt, the gun's metal warmed by her body heat. More weapons, smuggled out of Barcelona by Señora Ballester, were hidden in the now eerily silent convent and in shepherd's huts farther up in the mountains. Most in this village of fervent anarchists blindly believed Franco's Nationalist forces would never take Catalonia. Maria Raurell did not share that belief. She was a realist first. (In a year, and almost to the day, she would be proved right, but hardly comforted by it.)

The muffled dawn was cold and still. Patches of snow dotted the small clearing. She smelled the pinewood of the nearby coffin. Her feet were numb with cold but her skin felt like damp rubber and the world looked sharply black and white. Her senses seemed heightened, probably by the near-ness of death.

For a moment, Señora Raurell glanced back through the cork and pine trees at the village, where thin streamers of smoke rose like a ghostly host from the chimneys. The busi-ness of the day had begun but no one had yet left the meager warmth of the cottages. The sound of the gunshots would carry far; sound always did in the still mountain air. She was glad. All would know she'd carried out her duty as acting mayor on this, Saint Agatha's Day, the one day of the year when women ruled and men stayed home to perform do-mestic chores. Never mind that politics currently overruled religious observances, it was a special day for women, hark-ening far back to a time when women *did* rule.

She sighed deeply. War made people do strange things. Since Señora Ballester had been denounced by the cacique, the village political boss, Señora Raurell had thought a lot about what she was about to do—*had* to do. And now, she didn't need to think anymore.

She turned back around, aimed, and fired three shots directly into the heart. While waiting for the ringing in her ears to cease, she watched the blood soak into a patch of snow here, the hard earth there.

She went to the new coffin and took out the hammer and nails. With some effort, she placed the body in the coffin and nailed the lid shut. The grave had been dug the previous day. Now she would bring three women back to carry the coffin down to the cemetery. The cacique had argued against burial in hallowed ground; he had wanted the body left for the wolves. What did he know about hallowed ground? He'd led the others through the tunnel into the convent to mas-sacre the nuns in their sleep! His crudity and sense of political expediency disgusted Maria, but in the end he'd been outvoted. After all, Señora Ballester had done good things for their village. There would be no special grave marker, only a crude little cross as befitted a traitor. Later, Señora Raurell mused, she would remedy *that*, too.

Such a stupid man; he never goes to the graveyard anyway, Señora Raurell thought while hurrying down the slope, unaware that another pair of eyes had seen the execution. The child stepped into the clearing. She smeared the blood with a small fingertip, then slipped back into the forest.

CHAPTER ONE

The Present

". . . es Jesucrist, el Redemtor del mon."

The 727 landed with a jolt and a skid at Barcelona's Prat de Llobregat airport. A deafening roar filled the cabin as the engines reversed, inspiring yet another layered chorus of Spanish curses and prayers. Easily interpretable Catholic decades loudly voiced by the man fingering a rosary to Queenie Davilov's right, joined what must have been a Catalan hymn sung by the woman behind her:

Cedre gentil del Libano corona,
Arbre d'encens, Palmera de Sion,
el fruit sagrat que vostre amor ens dona,
es Jesucrist, el Redemtor del mon.

That was just one of many begun soon after they encountered the first air pocket out of Barajas airport on Madrid's

5

high plain. Delayed for three hours by a frightful storm, the passengers had applauded when the pilot finally announced their departure. But when the aircraft hit that first air pocket just minutes after takeoff, quite a few wished they'd taken the train.

For over an hour they rose and fell eastward in a sky not unlike a stormy sea.

Numbly, Queenie stared at the laminated Jim Rice baseball card imbedded in her palm as her body strained against the seat belt. Soon after leaving Los Angeles, she'd pulled it from her wallet when the captain suggested they keep their seat belts fastened while "we pass through some spring weather."

"Spring weather," she had discovered, was pilotese for severe turbulence. And the first heart-stopping plunge of five thousand feet—the distance determined by the Cassandra sitting beside her—had sent her rooting around her wallet for the baseball card her younger brother Rex had given her last year.

A facsimile had been found clutched in the hand of a small boy who'd survived a horrific airplane crash in an Iowa cornfield. At least to certain baseball players like her brother Rex, the Jim Rice card shared stature with other icons said to protect the traveler. Doubling her chances, Queenie had sought further consolation from the small Willendorf goddess swathed in silk in her satchel.

The roar abruptly fell to a purr. Now that their mission was successfully completed, Queenie returned the baseball card and squat little goddess to her satchel. At the same time, the singing behind her ceased and the man beside her dropped his rosary into his pocket. Whatever works, Queenie thought, and peered around him for her first sight of Barcelona—nothing more than lights studding a soft black background. Local time was nine thirty P.M.

Queenie breathed the stale recycled air, anxious to unfold her limbs and walk on terra firma again. With a sense of unease she hoped the lousy flight, one that would have made Torquemada proud, was not a precursor of things to come.

As the taxiing plane carried the passengers bobbing and swaying toward the terminal, the call from France that had sent her halfway around the world replayed in her head for the umpteenth time . . .

For the first minute or so, she'd listened to her agent, Eric Diamond, babble excitedly about too much champagne, too little sleep, thirty-dollar hot dogs, torturous screenings of multilingual films, and the general excitement of the Cannes Film Festival. Then he got to the point of the call.

"Got a job for you. Admittedly strange circumstances. You must get to . . . *I'll be right there, Charles. Champagne's on the sideboard.* Where was I?"

"You said I must get to—"

"Of course! Spain . . . Queenie. You there?"

"I'm not really awake. You said, Spain?"

"Hold on. What time is it?"

"Here in L.A. it's three A.M."

"Oh. Sorry . . . well, can't be helped. You simply must take this job. Frazier's an old friend. Money's good. Terrific, in fact. You must—*right there Charles!*"

"Eric. Please. Details."

"Digby Patterson has vanished off the face of the earth."

That name was certainly noteworthy, Digby Patterson being one of the most respected screenwriters in the business.

7

"So Patterson was working on a script for uh, Frazier when he . . . vanished?"

". . . fourth—or is this the fifth—doctoring job I've gotten you? Anyway, story concerns the Spanish civil war."

"Third, Eric."

"You did write a book didn't you?"

"What? About the Spanish civil war? Holy Mother, Eric, I told you once I made a short film—"

"Never mind. You're on." He then gave her the airline, flight number, and departure time. She heard a loud slurp, then he said, "There's something else. Hmmm. Can't remember. Too much of this bloody fantastic champagne. Oh well, it'll come to me. You'll collect your ticket at the ticket counter. Someone will meet the flight."

"What about a visa?"

"Visa? Not to worry. Just tell the authorities you're a tourist. I'm at the Carleton. If you need to get in touch I can't guarantee I'll be here or if I am, that I'll be sober enough to make sense. Bloody strange about Patterson. Good for your career though. No, *brilliant*. We'll have you in orbit yet. Well, I'm off now."

"Wait! Where in Spain am I going?"

"Oh. Right. Barcelona. Ta, love."

At least she had some knowledge of the Spanish civil war. In college, she'd made a short 16mm film about Dolores Ibarruri, dubbed la Pasionaria (the Passion Flower), a communist whose impassioned speeches helped seed the Spanish Republican army with the International Brigades, which included among its volunteers a number of literary figures. But what writer could resist a woman who, in defiance of Generalissimo Franco's fascist Nationalist party, fervently cried, "It is better to die on your feet than live on your knees!"

So, while champagne may have bloated a student film into a book, at least Eric remembered that Queenie had had *some* encounter with that part of Spain's history. A fact which probably had gotten her the job . . .

Finally, the aircraft came to a complete stop. The passengers exploded from their seats like popcorn hitting hot grease. Queenie followed suit, not bothering with polite amenities which, in any case, would have been useless given that the man in the window seat was all but climbing over her to get to the aisle.

With her satchel slung across her shoulder, Queenie joined the jostling herd, a soundtrack of bleats playing in her head.

Customs had been taken care of in Madrid. Having no bags to worry about, she felt an immediate sense of release and excitement overpowering the memory of her uncomfortable flight.

Just as quickly, the realization that she was alone in an unfamiliar country and unable to express herself beyond high school Spanish tore a chunk out of her spirit. She hadn't planned beyond reaching Barcelona itself, and suddenly experienced the scrambled brain sensation of panic. What if no one was there to meet her?

Regroup, Davilov, she told herself, deciding to do so in the nearest bar. Then she saw, to her relief, her name. It hung there, misspelled, the black letters suspended on a white background.

Panic vanished in her wake as she hurried toward the tall young man standing well behind the small crowd gathered to greet disembarking passengers. Her long black braid swung to the cadence of her stride. His unruly blond curls created a wildly rococo frame for a sunburned face in which were imbedded little black eyes. He lowered the sign as she approached, revealing NEW YORK YANKEES on the front of his T-shirt.

Her own proclaimed a certain allegiance to the Boston Red Sox. She further noted his faded denims and Docksiders worn without socks—American attire. If his shirt was any indication, he probably spoke a form of English.

"Hi," she announced. "I'm Queenie Davilov. With v's not f's."

He regarded her a moment then said in a nasal voice straight from the south shore of New Jersey, "Bad flight, huh."

She was slightly taken aback by his comment, then realized her appearance must have prompted the greeting. Well, so what, she thought. This isn't a blind date.

"Let's get your luggage and go."

She jogged to keep up as he hurried into the terminal. At five-ten, she was not physically intimidated by him and quickly met him stride for stride.

"No luggage," she said.

"They lose it?"

"No. All I brought was this." She patted her satchel. He didn't seem to notice.

"What's your name?"

"Nathan Arturo."

She started to thank him for waiting when he cavalierly tossed the sign behind a gigantic potted palm.

Queenie retrieved the sign. "I'd rather not have my name—even misspelled—on a large piece of litter."

"And I don't like waiting around half the night."

"Sorry about that. There was a terrible—"

"You can wait out front while I get the car."

Outside the terminal, Queenie filled her lungs with warm, balmy air stinking of exhaust fumes and vibrating with the nervous energy of impatient travelers; her first impression of Barcelona differed little from her last impression of Los Angeles. But anyone who allowed themselves to judge a destination by the airport surely would find the world disappointingly monochromatic.

A silver Jaguar sedan slid to a stop in front of her. She started to reach for the door, then saw Nathan behind the wheel on what, in the United States, is the passenger side. She stepped around the back end. Nathan leaned across the seat to open her door. She put the sign in the backseat, then climbed in beside him. To her irritation, he plucked the sign off the pale gray leather and tossed it out the window. Before she could protest, he shot out into traffic.

She took a few moments to compose herself, even managing a pleasant expression. "I gather you're working on the picture, Nathan, so what do you do?"

"A little bit of everything—Jesus! What's that smell?"

Bemused, she looked around the car's pristine interior. Then she realized she was the source of the noxious vapors, and flushed violently. She looked down at her jeans, then rolled down the window.

"I'd almost forgotten. A fellow passenger mistook my lap for a barf bag while we were spinning above Kansas. Unfortunately, airlines don't provide laundry facilities." She'd cleaned up as best she could, deciding against changing into her only other pair of jeans—anything that could happen once could happen twice.

11

He began to laugh, no doubt envisioning the scene. "I guess Nando didn't send you first class."

"You think first-class passengers don't puke? Anyway, I'm sorry about the smell. Guess I got used to it."

Nathan merged onto the *autovía*. There was little to see besides the ruby and diamond choker of traffic to and from the city, and the warmer yellow lights from tall stacks of apartment buildings.

"Who's Nando?"

"Señor Fernando Frazier," Nathan said dramatically.

"The director?"

"Slash producer."

"I got the impression he's British."

"He is."

"You called him 'señor.' "

"This is Spain, *mujer*."

And Fernando isn't exactly a British name, she wanted to say, but didn't. At least she remembered *mujer* translated to "woman." She wondered what the translation was for "asshole."

"I'm his personal assistant."

She began to wonder about Frazier. Anyone who'd choose such a disagreeable person for a personal assistant must be something of a misanthrope. Then she warned herself not to assume or prejudge. Still, the thought of working with anyone even remotely like Nathan made her uneasy.

"You know I'm the script doctor—"

"For now, anyway," he interrupted.

Why was he being such a jerk? "I mentioned that hoping you'd tell me something about the script."

He snorted. "Sure. You know what critics say about Antoni Gaudí's Sagrada Familia?"

"The cathedral, you mean?"

"The *unfinished* cathedral. And I quote, 'a grotesque, over-wrought mess.' "

That's nothing new, she told herself. The last script she'd doctored had required character surgery. Regardless of age or gender, the dialogue had sounded monotonously uniform. In four days she'd changed that. The first script had had no story, no cohesive foundation. Restructuring had taken two weeks, but she'd done it. If Nathan wanted to scare her off, he wasn't succeeding. But why would he want to?

"And the story?" she prompted.

Nathan heaved a sigh of exasperation. "Ever hear of the Spanish civil war?"

"Of course."

"Well?"

"Well what?"

"What do you know?"

"The last time I had a pop quiz was high school," she mumbled. But what if this was a test? If she couldn't come up with an answer, did Nathan have instructions to turn the car around and send her back to the United States?

"All right. The war began in nineteen thirty-six when Franco rolled out the red carpet to the Nazis, serving up cities like Guernica to test their weapons systems. This served a dual purpose by preparing Hitler for World War Two and aiding Franco with his civil problems. It ended in April nineteen thirty-nine." She paused then asked, "So, do I pass?"

In answer, he gave her a smug look.

Two can play this game, she thought. "Yes, nineteen thirty-nine was quite a year . . . and April quite a month. Especially at Yankee Stadium. But being a Yankees fan, you probably know all about that."

"About what?"

"Why don't you tell me."

He shot her an ugly look, then wrapped himself in a surly silence.

Queenie glanced out the window, suddenly aware that they'd entered the city proper. I must be jet-lagged, she thought, having allowed Nathan's acid personality to distract her. Deciding against giving him a short lesson in baseball history, she took in the sights.

This was not a city that went to bed early. All along the wide avenue, sidewalks were filled with window shoppers, families out for a stroll, and clusters of people at tables outside bars and cafés. Lights burned brightly in hotels and glass office buildings.

Nathan made a series of left and right turns until they gradually began to climb in a northwesterly direction. He'd become preoccupied with the time, checking his watch every few minutes, not bothering with any guide-style commentary. But she didn't expect him to be accommodating, and contented herself in absorbing the noisy scene on her own. All she wanted from him was to be dropped at her hotel.

One thing that struck her immediately was how stylishly everyone dressed. She was glad she'd thought to pack a good dress and pair of shoes along with more proletarian garb— the other pair of jeans and a couple of T-shirts.

Nathan made a right off an avenue she would come to know as Balmes, then a quick left up a narrow one-way street shadowed by multistory gray sandstone apartment buildings, many with small shops and bars on ground level. Near the top of the street, Nat pulled the Jaguar up onto the sidewalk and parked. She noticed that few cars were parked on the street itself, and those that were looked somewhat battered.

"Watch out for dogshit," he cautioned as they hurried toward the double glass door of what appeared to be an apartment house.

"Why are we stopping here?" she asked as he unlocked the door. "Am I going to meet Señor Frazier? Frankly, I'd like to clean up . . ."

He moved on without answering. They passed a bank of letter boxes, then turned a corner and entered an elevator before he answered.

"This is where you'll be staying."

He punched the button for the top floor, and they began the ascent to the *sobre ático*, experiencing a moment's anxiety when the light dimmed and the elevator slowed. Nathan pounded the button, then heaved a great sigh as the trip to the seventh floor resumed. The cab quickly filled with Queenie's unpleasant scent.

"What were you saying about the Yankees?" he asked nonchalantly.

"April nineteen thirty-nine."

"What of it?"

"Lou Gehrig's last at bat, Ted Williams's first. Of course, Ted Williams was with the Red Sox."

A modicum of interest appeared in his otherwise insolent face. "So, how'd they do?" He looked surprised when she answered.

"Gehrig went oh for four. Williams struck out." She felt annoyed with herself. Sure, two can play but it doesn't make the game any less foolish. She'd have to be careful around Nathan. He brought out parts of herself she didn't like.

The moment the doors began to part, Nathan dashed out.

Queenie followed, noting that there were only two apartments separated by a wide polished granite landing.

Nat unlocked the door of the apartment on the right, and switched on the light. Queenie entered and faced her reflection in the flocked gold floor-to-ceiling mirror that formed one wall of an elegant foyer. Inwardly she groaned. But what did she expect after hours in aero hell? Her clothes were dingy and stained, her eyes appeared to be a fuzzy red, and her hair looked like she'd washed it in chewing gum.

She set her satchel on a long bent-legged table and turned her attention to a couple of publications beside a green cut-glass vase containing a spray of fresh yellow daffodils. Along with the flowers, someone had thought to leave today's *International Herald Tribune* and a Spanish guide to Barcelona's attractions. Beneath them was another copy of the *Herald Tribune*—oddly, last Monday's edition.

Then a voice, definitely not Nat's, startled her. "Who's there?"

She looked around but Nat had disappeared. In the scarce minute since they'd entered, he seemed to have vanished. Had he simply left without giving her a key?

"Hello?" she called out nervously.

Suddenly Nat reappeared, shooting out of a small room off the foyer. Before she could wonder what he'd been doing, she heard the sound of bare feet slapping against the granite floor. Then a large man appeared, with a maroon towel clutched at his waist. His face was lathered but for a couple of paths in the foam down his left cheek. The wet hair on his head stuck out like spikes on a mace.

"You're fired, Andrew," Nathan said abruptly.

"What?"

The man, Andrew, appeared to have just been struck across the face. Queenie tensed at this unexpected and potentially combustible situation.

"I said you're fired. History. Nando wants you off the project."

"Now just a bloody minute!" Andrew advanced a step. His eyes shifted and for the first time he noticed Queenie. "Who the hell's this?"

"Your replacement."

"This is a joke," Andrew snapped. Abruptly turning, he slapped back down the hall. "If you and your tart want a place to fuck, get a hotel."

Emotions began to itch just beneath her skin: anger, embarrassment, shock, and the fear that somewhere she'd made a wrong turn.

"I mean it, Andrew," Nathan called out. "Pack your stuff and get out."

Andrew reappeared, the towel gripped so tightly Queenie could see his knuckle bones bleached in tension. Though he was half-naked, he still looked capable of murder. For the moment, Queenie simply watched the minidrama unfold.

"I'm calling Frazier!"

"He's still in France. And anyway, he's the one who fired you."

"I can't believe this!"

Nathan glanced quickly at his watch. "You've got a return ticket and you can't stay here anymore."

Unable to contain himself any longer, Andrew suddenly grabbed Nathan's T-shirt, crushing the Yankees. "If I find out this is some scheme of yours, I'll kill you, you worthless twit." Then with a violent shove, he released Nathan, who stumbled backward, nearly falling. At least Nathan had the good sense to scoot around the open door.

"I'll sue you for that!" he yelled and ran back to the elevator.

Queenie dashed after him, holding back the elevator door. "Wait a minute! You can't just leave me—"

"Be ready at eight tomorrow morning. Now move out of the way."

"I need a key and a copy of the script," she blurted, her mind racing. What else did she need?

"Tell Andrew to give you his."

"You don't mean to tell me this is the first he knew about being replaced?" Such cavalier treatment of a fellow scribe shocked her. She'd heard some horror stories but up until now thought they were exaggerations. "What if he hadn't been here? And then come back later—"

"I would have found him, now get out of the way!"

Queenie didn't move. Nathan violently punched the elevator button.

"Where can I get money changed?"

Nathan reached in his pocket and tossed a wad of bills onto the landing. With a sigh, she moved to pick up the money. The door slid shut.

Andrew will give me his, all right.

Queenie returned to the apartment, leaving the door open in case she might need to make a fast exit.

"Hello?" she called out tentatively and took a step toward the dark hallway. Immediately to the right was a small room, furnished spartanly with a narrow metal-framed bed and a table and chair. The table, used as a desk, sat beside a tall closed window. Papers were scattered around a laptop computer. Behind the chair was a built-in cupboard with shelves and drawers.

Behind a closed door at the end of the hall she could hear cursing and banging. Deciding on the side of prudence, she moved back into the foyer. She felt enough like an intruder already without having him catch her checking out his work area.

She glanced down the other hallway figuring it probably led to the living room. She would have liked to have a look around, but that could wait. Andrew was mad enough simply to leave before giving her the keys. She sighed and stayed by the door.

She didn't have long to wait. He stormed into the foyer. With barely a glance at her, he dropped a large suitcase and hanging bag, then disappeared into the small study, slamming the door behind him. By the amount of luggage he had, he'd obviously planned on staying a while.

A few moments later, he came out carrying the laptop packed in its travel case, and a sheaf of papers. He began stuffing the papers in his hanging bag.

"Bloody bastard's gone?"

"Left a few minutes ago."

"You're American?"

Queenie nodded. "You need to call a cab?"

He shook his head and zipped up the bag.

"Uh, Nathan said I could have your keys."

While shouldering the hanging bag, he pulled a key ring from his pocket and tossed it onto the table. Then, gathering his other luggage, and without another word, he stormed out of the apartment.

Queenie closed the door and stood digesting the whole

scene for a few minutes. Then she remembered the script and pulled the door back open. The landing was empty, the elevator gone.

"Shit," she mumbled as she slammed the door. Bad flight, unpleasant arrival—what next?

CHAPTER TWO

ANDREW MUST HAVE taken the soap. *All* the soap. She could find neither a bar nor a sliver in the bathroom or in the elaborate complex of closets and cupboards in an adjacent hallway leading to another bedroom. She did find fresh towels, though, and used the shampoo she'd brought from home, Mane n' Tail, a preparation designed for horses, to wash both hair and body. So what if she shopped at the tack-and-feed store for beauty supplies? The products worked just as well on humans.

The tub was quite large and located in the far left-hand corner of the windowless bathroom. There was no curtain nor a rod to hold one.

Unlike American showers, this one consisted of a spoonbill-shaped showerhead affixed to a snaking stainless steel tube embedded in the tub near the faucets. The neck was held in place by a clip high on the tile wall, and could be removed if anyone chose to sit in the tub and hand-hold it to wash their hair. One added feature, and not entirely welcome, was that it moved according to water pressure—or some quirky design. One had to sort of dance beneath it. At one point when she turned the hot water to full, the showerhead reared back and shot a stream into the doorway fully five feet away.

But once she'd mastered the idiosyncrasies, she felt the smells and strain of her journey vanish. By the time her body was lotioned (with Udder Butter) and wrapped in a short cotton kimono, and her hair combed into a black silken sheet, she felt much like a new hatchling with exploration and settling in on its mind.

She found herself to be the lone occupant (so far) of a three-bedroom apartment. The two back bedrooms faced the street and shared a narrow terrace. The third bedroom was the one Andrew had used as a study. She entered and switched on the light.

The bulb behind the fixture in the ceiling offered little illumination. She opened the casement window beside an ordinary table and peered down a lightwell to a littered patch seven stories below. Laughter, music, and Spanish gibberish filtered up from the lower-level apartments. She closed the window and turned to the adjacent built-in shelves and drawers.

A portable manual typewriter, an anachronism in the computer age, sat on the lower shelf. In a drawer she found a stack of cheap paper and a pen with FOREVER embossed on it. She tested the thin foam mattress on the bed. But whether it was the long drop down the shaft, or the lousy lighting, she didn't like the room. It felt creepy—or maybe she was responding to some angry spoor left by Andrew.

She'd just turned out the light when a buzzer blared insistently. She hurried into the foyer, where she'd seen an intercom beside the door.

"Yes?" she answered tentatively, wondering how she'd respond if someone started speaking Spanish.

"Andrew here."

"Oh. You forget something?"

"Indeed. My manners. Look, would you like to go for a drink?"

Queenie hesitated. While Andrew might not be the best company at the moment, she did want his copy of the script.

"The least I can do is show you round the neighborhood," he said.

"Okay. Just give me a few minutes to get dressed."

"There's a bar at the top of street, on the left. Casa Carmella. I'll meet you there."

She started to ask if he wanted to leave his things in the apartment, but he'd already gone. Anyway, he'd probably spent the past thirty minutes or so finding a hotel—in which case, he'd decided to stay. Why? she wondered.

CHAPTER THREE

A TALL BLACK woman with an Afro dominated the bar, which ran from beside the open door to the far wall. Six tiny tables with two chairs each were behind the bar stools. Andrew sat on the first stool by the door. The bartender leaned across the bar talking to him. She straightened when Queenie crossed the threshold. At the same time, Andrew moved off the stool and guided Queenie to a table against the far window.

The lighting was bright and quite harsh. The patrons seemed to be locals, people well at ease with each other, an equal mix of men and women. There was no music or television to distract from the purpose of neighbors coming together to drink and talk. Behind the bar were half a dozen cheaply framed eight-by-ten glossies of a showgirl wearing elaborate headdresses and skimpy sequined and beaded costumes.

"Now, what would you like?"

"Beer's fine."

"May I suggest the Vol Damm. It's stronger than American beer, and quite good."

As he placed the order at the bar, she took the opportunity to really look at him for the first time. He was better-looking than her first impression, when anger had distorted his features. Now he was calm and his collar-length brown hair neatly combed. She sensed he was older than he looked, good genes having preserved him from the general deterioration that accompanied a long writing career. His clothes were well cut and he had a good tan. Maybe he'd been fired for spending too much time sunbathing instead of writing.

"Cheers," he said after sitting down and pouring for both of them.

"Cheers," Queenie said and took a drink. The beer was bitter and cold. "You're right. The beer's good."

"I really must apologize for my appalling behavior."

"Is that really the first you'd heard about being fired?"

"Yes. I'd no idea. Bloody hell, I've only been here a couple of days! So, let's start over." He extended his hand. "Andrew Coachman."

"Queenie Davilov." She smiled. "I take it you're not leaving."

"Ah." He glanced toward the bar. "Carmella's putting me up for a few days. Thought I'd at least finish my holiday. You see, I was in Malta when my agent called. Been there about ten days. Said he had a quick-and-dirty job for me. And I'd make enough to cover holiday expenses and then some." He sighed, then raised his eyebrows and shrugged.

Well, she thought, that explains all the luggage and the

tan. She repeated what Nathan had said about the script being "an overwrought mess."

"Encouraging, isn't he? Fancies himself a writer; no doubt incapable."

"If Digby Patterson had to work with him, I can understand why he walked off the picture. Did you know him?"

"Digs? Known him donkey's years. We were even flatmates once. Back in London in the sixties. A great time, that." Then he asked about her credits. That didn't take long. She asked about his, and recognized the titles of several British films and a *Masterpiece Theatre* series.

He regarded her with some skepticism. "All I can say is, you must have a bloody good agent."

Queenie had to agree, somewhat baffled that a writer with his professional background would be replaced by a relative novice like herself. She decided to change the subject.

"So what do you think happened to Digby Patterson?"

"Haven't a clue. I know he's had liver problems in recent years. Rather a hard drinker, our Digs. Could be he simply checked into a hospital."

"Surely he'd tell someone."

"Yes," he said thoughtfully. "Not like Digs at all to simply walk off like that."

They sipped their beers for a moment. Then Queenie resumed the conversation.

"Nathan said I could have your script."

"Oh, he did, did he? Well, I'll keep it if you don't mind!" Then he smiled slightly. "Sorry. Look, let me show you the neighborhood. Do me good to walk off some of this temper."

As they strolled along the narrow sidewalk, occasionally having to step into the street to pass parked cars, Andrew pointed out the *panadería* where she could buy fresh bread, the *papellería*, which sold writing supplies, and the best tapas bars. He said one could make a meal of assorted small portions of seafood, fried croquettes, salads, and tortillas—the latter being omelettes, the most popular of which were cooked with potatoes.

He told her about the hours, that most shops closed between one and four, then stayed open until around eight; that between seven A.M. and two A.M. she wouldn't have to leave the block to find something to eat or drink. He showed her the bodega, stocked with massive casks, where he bought wine and had once shared a glass with the gregarious owner.

"Don't get him talking about politics, though. In fact, don't talk politics to *any* Catalonian. A good number of them don't believe they're really part of Spain."

"Given the state of my Spanish, or should I say Spanglish, that won't be a problem."

"Ah, you'd be surprised at your fluency after a few glasses of wine."

Finally, they came back to Carmella's. This time he introduced Queenie to the proprietor, who, he mentioned, had been a showgirl in Cuba. Carmella regarded Queenie with a stony expression.

"If you're interested in Cuban cigars, Carmella's the one to see," Andrew said.

"I'll remember that," Queenie replied, wondering if she should add cigars to her other tobacco vices.

"*Tu suerte!*" Carmella suddenly demanded, grabbing Queenie's wrist.

"What?"

Andrew smiled. "She wants to read your palm. Tell your fortune."

For a moment, Carmella studied Queenie's outstretched

right hand, concluding the reading by closing the fingers over the palm. Then she whispered something to Andrew and, after an angry glance at Queenie, moved away to pour drinks for another customer.

"Well?" Queenie asked.

"She says you're a spy—here to spy on people."

Queenie shrugged. "I suppose that's one way of looking at a writer."

"And that death brought you here."

"She's batting a thousand. After all, what is war about if not death? In this case, the Spanish civil war."

But not wanting to be rude, she turned to the bartender. "*Gracias*, Carmella, uh, *para mi suerte.*" Carmella's expression did not soften. The woman clearly did not like Queenie.

Queenie thanked Andrew for the beer and the tour; now she wanted to get some sleep.

"Look, I might as well tell you," he said before they parted for the night. "I'm not leaving until I have a word with Frazier."

"Andrew," she said, "the fact that I'm here pretty well proves that you've been replaced. You don't really believe Nathan was just being spiteful?"

"Frankly, I'm going to lobby to get the job back. This sort of dismissal isn't good for one's reputation."

"Hmm."

"But do watch out for Nathan," he added quickly. "The second night I was here, I caught him rooting around the study, going through my work. This was about two in the morning. Anyway, I grabbed him by the hair and flung him out." He sighed. "Could be that's what cost me the job. Anyway, be careful. Remember he's got a key to the flat."

"Well thanks for the warning—*both* warnings," she added pointedly.

She walked quickly back to the apartment, wondering if Andrew would get the job back. At this point, there was only one thing she felt certain about: There would be none of Carmella's Cuban cigars in her future.

CHAPTER FOUR

DICK TAKAHASHI, QUEENIE'S boyfriend and featured player in her dream, sauntered up the aisle of an enormous airplane. He pulled his shirt out of his trousers, moving ever closer to her seat. He began to unbutton his shirt. The shirt turned into a bird and flew away. Delighted, she wondered if the same thing would happen to his trousers. The muscled fabric of his skin was almost within reach. She started to get up and touch him—when suddenly a filthy bandage appeared on his head and he began speaking urgently, and oddly, with a British accent.

"Do wake up!"

She struggled with half-open eyelids weighted by fatigue. A part of her stubbornly refused to leave Dick. Then she felt an all-too-real hand on her shoulder. Her eyes shot open and a scream locked in her throat.

The room was in darkness but for the faint glow from the hallway silhouetting the apparition bending over her. A dirty, blood-stained bandage circled his head. From beneath it shone a pair of intense eyes. He straightened and she saw he wore a greasy, blue, piecemeal uniform. The only tidy aspect of his appearance was a sooty bullet hole in the jacket's breast pocket. This was not Dick Takahashi. Nor was this man likely to be alive.

"You're damned hard to wake up. For a moment, I thought you were going to kiss me. Well, never mind. Come on, we need to talk."

She swallowed the scream and sat up. "Who the hell are you? What time is it?"

"Half four. I'm Freddie."

"As in Krueger?" She was only half-jesting. Evil Freddy Krueger attacked people in their sleep.

A smile softened his eyes. "Get dressed. I'll meet you on the terrace. And be quick. There's a good girl."

She dressed and used the bathroom. After shampooing her face and rinsing in cold water, she felt more awake, and gratefully rid of the dream's sexual residue. The apartment was cold so she retrieved the comforter, then, wrapped in its warmth, swept out to the front terrace where light from the living room crept uncertainly along the slightly damp terra-cotta tiles.

Stars burned tiny holes in the velvety sky. Freddie stood at the railing smoking a cigarette. Beyond him a few lights were on in the otherwise black bowl formed by the surrounding buildings. An insulated carafe and two cups were on the table. She smelled coffee and remembered a brown bag of fresh ground she'd found in the refrigerator when she checked out the kitchen.

At the sound of her approach, he turned. With his cigarette dangling from his lips, he poured and handed her a cup.

She sat down. He pulled a silver flask from his jacket and added a healthy dollop to his cup.

"Brandy?"

"No thanks. Too early—or is it too late?"

"Neither. To locals, anyway. They drink *café carajillo* at all hours." He set the flask between them. Their images were faint and distorted on its silver surface.

"Excuse me if I'm a little slow right now. You're Freddie . . . ?"

"Frazier. The director."

Slash producer. The revelation had the effect of a shot of caffeine on Queenie but it was Freddie who suddenly got up and peeked around the ten-foot-high partition that separated this terrace from its neighbor. Apparently satisfied that no eavesdroppers were about, he returned to his chair.

"Well, you'd best sharpen up, seeing as how you have two jobs."

"What?"

"Surely Eric told you?"

"Told me what?"

He made a little liquid sound then sat straighter in the chair. "I see. Well, let's get to the point. I'm due to set up a shoot before first light. Thought I'd pop over while we have privacy."

"Is there a problem?" Her hands tightened around her cup.

He gave her a look that suggested what she'd said was understatement in the extreme.

"We all know Murphy's Law is the foundation of film-making," he began.

Anything that can go wrong will flashed through Queenie's mind. "Sure."

"Well, I'm afraid it's rather beyond that now. Someone, I fear, is out to sabotage me. I'm going to be honest with you, Queenie—may I call you Queenie?"

"Of course."

"Yes, well, you weren't so much hired for your writing talent as for your experience as a private investigator."

He watched her carefully as she absorbed the truth. She recalled Andrew's statement—*"You must have a bloody good agent"*—when they both tried to figure out why she'd been called to replace a writer of his stature. Then she remembered something else: *"She says you're a spy—here to spy on people."*

"Eric said you were responsible for solving that sensational murder in Hollywood last year."

"Well, I'd been working as a script supervisor for—"

Freddie waved his hand impatiently. "Yes, yes. No need to go into your curriculum vitae. Eric already told me you moonlight between film jobs as an investigator."

"May I have one of your cigarettes?"

So this was the "something else" Eric couldn't quite remember.

He reached into the pocket of his frayed jacket and brought out a red and gold box of Dunhills. With a gold lighter he lit hers and another for himself.

She inhaled deeply, feeling more awake. "Do you always dress like that?"

He laughed. "Much worse, actually." After a pause he explained. "On occasion, some of the extras have shown up at the wrong place. If I need one, I'm it. Another annoyance." He sipped his coffee, then continued.

"I always go to Cannes whether I'm in production or not. Eric and I have a standing date. After telling him about the problems I've been having, he said he had the perfect writer. Not only could you write but you could help me find out who might be behind these problems. Believe me, I jumped at the chance even though you're not an established name."

"Well, if you get the urge to fire me, please don't use Nathan Arturo as the messenger. It might result in justifiable homicide." To illustrate her point, she sketched the scene she'd witnessed between Andrew Coachman and Nathan.

Freddie sighed eloquently. "Nathan should have taken care of that before your arrival. You see, I only just returned from Cannes several hours ago. The film's been in hiatus for a week—while I attended the film festival. Anyway, when it appeared Digs might not be returning, I brought Andrew onto the project." He paused. "Apparently Digs walked off sometime between last Friday night and Saturday morning. You know him?"

"I met him once."

"Well, for him to leave a project unfinished is completely out of character."

"Are you telling me you suspect foul play?"

"I don't know what to think. You see, we were having problems with the script. Quite suddenly, he said we had to trash the ending, that it was all wrong. Unfortunately, he wouldn't tell me what he had in mind. . . . My going off to France gave him the opportunity to work out the story problems. So, on the one hand, you see, I wasn't worried upon first learning that no one had seen him for several days; simply figured he was off doing research."

He stopped and checked his watch. She sensed he wanted to bring this conversation to a conclusion. "What I need is someone on the inside. You know how film families are. If I went to the police or hired an outside investigator, everyone would be suspicious, the culprit, if there is one, on guard. Being the writer, you're free to ask questions with no one suspecting your motives."

Queenie remained silent, hoping the investigative work would neatly and simply overlap the script-doctoring job. Unfortunately, something told her nothing about this film was neat or simple.

"Insurance premiums skyrocketed after we lost a lorry full of equipment, and later when the cast came down with food poisoning. Then there are the small things like extras showing up down by the harbor when they're supposed to be outside the city."

He finished his coffee and tucked the flask back into his jacket. "Now I must be off."

"Wait a minute," she said, standing with him. "What about money?"

"Ah! Your fee. Double whatever you normally charge for such endeavors. I'll direct my bank in London to deposit the money into your account in California. You can give me the particulars later. As for ready cash . . ." He pulled out a wallet and handed her a short stack of five-thousand-peseta notes.

With the money crushed in her hand, she followed him through the living room and into the lighted foyer. "Thanks, but I was actually referring to Digby Patterson. Had he been paid in full?"

He turned. Now in bright light, she could see he was older than she'd first thought, well into his fifties.

"Oh. I see. Well, he'd received two-thirds and was due the final third when the film wrapped."

"So I am the script doctor?" She needed the verbal confirmation.

"Yes, er, of course," he replied after a slight hesitation that made her uneasy. But maybe he was just preoccupied.

"Well I need a script, don't I?"

"Nathan didn't give you one?"

"No. He said I could have Andrew's. Then Andrew refused to give me his—said he was going to try and get the job back."

"Well, not to worry. The job's yours."

She managed a smile.

"We'll discuss the story on the coach."

"The coach?"

"Later, when we're off to the location, northwest of Gerona. You'll need to pack your gear." He reached for the doorknob.

"Have you got a computer for me to work on? I noticed Andrew had a laptop."

"Funny you should mention it, bloody thing blew up. Faulty transformer or something. Electricity in this country is not to be trusted."

"Maybe I should bring the typewriter."

"Typewriter?

"The one in the study."

He seemed momentarily confused.

"Ah, the typewriter. Yes, of course. I'll send someone round to collect you later. We're scheduled to leave at noon."

"Nathan said someone would pick me up at eight."

"Fine. Just one more thing. All these accidents could well be organic—simply the natural result of making a film on foreign soil. And Digs might be off someplace so immersed in the work he's lost track of time. You know how writers are—though I think he might have at least rung me. Still, as Ian Fleming wrote, 'First time happenstance, second time circumstance, third time enemy action.' Not a word about this to anyone, and don't speak to me of it unless we're quite alone."

"All right."

"Do forgive me for waking you, and try to get some sleep. Remember, you're going to be doubly busy for the next few days."

CHAPTER FIVE

AND DEATH BROUGHT *you here.*

Carmella's singular prophecies clouded Queenie's mood as she leaned against the terrace railing, surveying her temporary backyard in the morning sun.

Seven stories below, white-clad members of the tennis club, mostly women, thunked balls on the clay courts, palms and assorted evergreens insulating them in this residential oasis. Off to the east, a wedge of the Mediterranean could be seen between the densely packed buildings that swept down to the harbor. Since sunrise she'd seen the sea's color shift from the deep green of a ripe avocado to bright aqua. The clouds were gone, swept away by the early morning breeze and now, at a little after eight, the sky was a vast, imperfect blue.

Unable to sleep after Freddie left, she had hung out her clothes on the line on the back terrace. Last night she'd tossed them into the small washer in the kitchen before going to bed, believing at the time that she'd be staying at the apartment.

She topped off her cup from the refilled carafe on the table. Of course death brought me here, she thought, trying to reassure herself. War is mass murder; this particular one was spiked with lies and betrayal.

She sat down and picked up the book she'd brought from home, a copy of *Goddess Sites: Europe*, by Anneli S. Rufus and Kristan Lawson. After the job concluded she wanted to spend a week or two touring, maybe even stop in London to see her twin brother, Raj. She turned to the section on Spain and began reading, but her mood was not conducive to concentration. In a moment the book was back on the table.

Glancing to the west, she regarded the statue of Christ high atop the cathedral on Mount Tibidabo, his arms raised and wide, poised to embrace the city. She recognized it from the 1992 Summer Olympics, which she'd watched as much for their travelogue value as for the competitions.

Her thoughts slipped back to Digby Patterson. She could find no sensible reason that a writer of his stature would suddenly go AWOL. But she had to admit that his absence had roughly opened the door for her—a doctoring job on a major production could well lead to the sale of one of her screenplays.

Laughter and then a distressed shout in Spanish rose above the thunks of tennis balls. Queenie got up and looked down. Close to the net, a woman was being helped to her feet. She'd probably vaulted the net in triumph only to land on her bottom. *Hubris*, Queenie mused, and decided to cease speculation on future success.

Behind her the sliding doors were open so she'd hear the

buzzer. Though he had a key, she doubted Nathan would make the effort to come up.

She sat down and resumed reading.

At nine o'clock she rolled a couple of cigarettes, wondering if she'd gotten the time wrong. Nathan had said eight o'clock, hadn't he? Maybe he was stuck in traffic. She lit a cigarette—a trick that used to work in restaurants to bring a delayed meal. Now, though, with smoking bans, such an act would be relegated to social history. Would meals then never arrive? Would Nathan?

During the next hour, as the sun continued its steady climb, so too did Queenie's anxiety. Finding concentration again difficult, she put down the book. Then she heard someone moving on the adjoining terrace.

"No! Es too dangerous! Please, Ian, donut ask me again!"

Queenie waited for Ian's reply. When none was forthcoming, the woman resumed in heavily accented English:

"When ar baby es born, he weel know—*caga!*" There was a pause after the sharp curse. "Of course I love you, but do not you see, when the baby es born, he weel know it ees not mine—*hes!* Hes!"

Intrigued, Queenie got up and peeked around the partition. In profile, a young woman wearing a pink bathrobe, her black hair in rollers, seemed to be addressing a tall potted palm. While certainly a healthy plant, it didn't have the equipment necessary to impregnate the woman speaking to it.

Suddenly, the woman jerked her head toward Queenie and jumped slightly. She screeched angrily in Spanish.

"Sorry, I couldn't help overhearing," Queenie said.

The woman disappeared into the apartment.

Queenie returned to the table. She resented being cooped

up on her first day in Spain. She checked her watch again. Ten twenty. Freddie had said they were leaving for the location at noon. Had she been forgotten? She had just resumed her seat when the buzzer went off.

"Finally!" she exclaimed and hurried into the foyer and pressed the intercom.

"Hello?"

But the voice that answered did not come through the intercom, nor was it Nathan's. Queenie had mistaken the doorbell for the intercom buzzer.

A woman shouted something in Spanish. Queenie peered through the peephole, and saw her neighbor on the other side—the woman's angry face, all nose with cheeks dropping to the sides in the fish-eye lens.

The shouting resumed the moment the door began to open.

"Excuse me," Queenie said, shaking her head. "I don't understand. Uh, *no comprende.*"

The woman stopped for a moment and blinked. Then she blurted, *"Donde está Andreu?"*

"Andreu?" Then she understood. "Andrew! Where's Andrew." Queenie bit her lip. "Uhmm." Then she shook her head. "No here. Uh, *aquí no.* Andrew. *Nada.*" She was beginning to sweat.

The woman made a mighty gesture of exasperation, flinging up her hands and spouting more angry Spanish. Several curlers fell to the floor.

"Yes, I know. I'd hate to be trying to talk to me, too. But I just heard you speaking English. Why won't you use it now?"

The woman poked her chest several times. Then she waved her hands toward herself. "Go 'way!" Suddenly, she spun around and stormed back to her apartment, slamming the door. Queenie picked up the curlers and, crossing the landing, left them outside the woman's door.

Queenie returned to the terrace, though her neighbor did not. For the next thirty minutes or so, Queenie alternately fumed at Nathan and tried to construct a plan in case he should not show. It was like being lost: the best course of action was no action at all. Both Freddie and Nathan knew her location, so she'd best stay put. However, at the point when waiting became intolerable she would leave a note on the apartment house door saying she was up the street at Carmella's. Hopefully, Andrew would be there. Since he planned to get the job back, he'd probably know where to reach Freddie Frazier.

What if Nathan had meant eight P.M.? What if Nathan had been fired? What if Freddie's visit had all been a dream?

The temperature dropped suddenly as a cloud cut in front of the sun, with fat gray friends tagging behind. She shivered and at the same time heard an odd shuffling sound behind her.

"Nice of the architect to give Jesus the best view in the city."

Badly startled, she jerked around. The voice came from a most extraordinary person. Had she been at the railing, instead of sitting at the table absently staring at Tibidabo, chances were good she'd have fallen over the side and ruined someone's tennis match.

CHAPTER SIX

"'THE SPANISH COULDN'T imagine Jesus being tempted in the desert. More appropriate that the devil choose this mountain, highest in the Collserola. You'll find the passage in Saint Matthew: *'Haec omnia tibi dabo si cadens adoraberis me.'* Simply, 'This is all yours if you worship me.' Or something like that. Makes sense, don't you think? I know I'd not be the least bit interested in kowtowing to someone who offered a mere a patch of sand in return. Surely the devil isn't that cheap."

The speaker stood about six feet tall and was dressed much as Freddie had been, though this man's uniform was brown and, if possible, even dirtier. His hair was matted and crusty with blood on one side. His blue eyes were red-rimmed. A narrow scar ran from the corner of his generous mouth to a deep dimple in his dirt-smudged left cheek. His feet were wrapped in filthy rags tied with string.

"And given the sacking of the churches and murders of priests and nuns by the anarchists during the civil war, you have to marvel at Jesus's powers of forgiveness. But, when Judgment Day comes, I think he'll slap the hands of the Catholic Church for siding with the fascists and monarchists in the first place. Considering the outright destruction of Guernica and Huesca—not to mention the University City in Madrid—I think Barcelona fared pretty well." He shrugged. "But who knows, maybe Jesus simply had a fondness for the Sagrada Familia, and wanted nothing to happen to it—including its completion."

He finally stopped talking.

"Who are you?"

Color infused his face. "Michael deBeers." He offered a smile, but no handshake, which was just as well. His hands appeared to have been dipped in a mixture of blood and motor oil. Then a frown made dirty lines in his forehead. "You're the writer, aren't you?"

"Queenie Davilov."

"Nathan sent me to collect you."

"Three hours off target."

"Sorry?"

"He told me someone would be here at eight."

"Oh. He gave me his keys, what, twenty, thirty minutes ago? I came straightaway."

"Look, the history lesson was nice, but what do you say we get going?" She slung the satchel over her shoulder, then suddenly remembered the clothes on the back terrace.

"I'll meet you at the elevator," she said hurrying past him. "I just need to get my clothes off the line."

A moment later, she stepped outside and locked the door. Toting the typewriter, and with her now dry clothes over one arm, she joined him at the elevator, where they listened to the gears as the cab slowly ascended.

"You're American, right?"

"Right."

"Well, don't be offended, but there's time and then there's Spanish time."

Queenie didn't reply until the doors slid open and they entered the elevator. She pushed the *bajo* button. While descending she tried to muster a degree of good humor to cancel the greater part of her anger at Nathan. No fair to take it out on this poor soldier.

"So which side are you on?"

"Neither anymore." He looked quite forlorn. "I'm dead now."

Her laugh died a moment later with the lights and the elevator. Michael muttered a curse then started pounding the buttons. Nothing happened. Queenie looked out the small pane of glass, her eyes level with the third floor landing. She would have liked to see a pair of shoes but no one was around.

Queenie fell back against the metal wall of their small prison. Michael appeared embarrassed, then resumed pounding the buttons. "Electricity must have gone off. It does that."

He looked over at her. "Do me a favor. Yell *'hola'* with me? I feel stupid doing it by myself."

"Sure. On three. One, two, three . . ."

"*Hola!*"

The volume of their chorus left them both stunned. Then they agreed to bang on the door together. Still, no one came. Finally, Michael sat down.

"Not settling in, are you?" she asked in alarm.

"Everyone's at work and the *portero* might not be in the building."

"*Portero?*"

"Collects the garbage, sees to the general maintenance. Anyway, we'd have to catch him at the right time. He lives in the building next door."

"How do you know that?"

"I used to live in the apartment where you're staying. Nathan and I were flatmates." He eyed her satchel. "You wouldn't happen to have food in there?"

"Michael, are you anticipating a long wait?" she asked anxiously.

He shrugged. "It's nearly lunchtime—which lasts until four or thereabouts."

Both were silent for a moment, then Queenie peered in her satchel. "If this was California, we'd have water, vitamins and Hershey's chocolate; we could write our memoirs, throw out a fishing line, and even have safe sex—but no. I cleaned it out before leaving L.A. Earthquakes, you know."

"Ah. We have floods in the Netherlands. More predictable, though."

"You're Dutch?"

"Yes."

"So what are you doing in Spain?"

"Got my MBA in Barcelona."

"Really? Why here?"

"The school's excellent—affiliated with Harvard Business School and Opus Dei."

"Opus Dei?"

"A darkly secret Catholic sect," he said in mock menace. "Means 'God's work.' Interesting bunch. They were kicked out of England at one time. Involved with Vatican business affairs. Into mortification of the flesh and that sort of thing. A couple of my professors even wore cilices; some have barbs to poke their thighs and remind them of sin.

"Anyway, I graduated last year. The school lets Señor Frazier use the facilities on weekends—which is why I'm dressed thusly. We've been shooting skirmishes since dawn."

Though Michael deBeers was a most agreeable person to be stuck with in an elevator, Queenie was due someplace else. "Look, if you don't mind, I'd like to get out of here. Let's keep trying to attract someone."

For a couple minutes they yelled and pounded on the door. But their efforts were in vain.

Finally, Michael said, "Maybe you'd be more comfortable sitting down. Give you more headroom."

She joined him on the floor. While they talked she folded her clothes and put them in the satchel.

"Don't worry, this happens all the time," he said.

"Elevators stopping of their own accord?"

He shrugged. "Who knows? This is Spain, after all. It's funny, in the cathedral in the Barrio Gótico—that's the oldest part of the city—is the chapel of—you'll never guess."

"I can't imagine."

"Our Lady of Electricity."

They stared at each other for a moment, then both laughed. Michael ran his fingers through his matted light brown hair, and with his arm wiped the sweat from his forehead. The move plus the dirt on his face seemed to emphasize the scar running from mouth to cheek, which she noticed was real. Oddly, it enhanced his looks, gave him a degree of character that his youth couldn't. He seemed to be about the age of her younger brother, Rex. Somewhere in his early twenties, a good nine years her junior.

"Not very effective, is she?" he said.

"Maybe no one's figured out if she's AC or DC."

They shared another laugh. While he was most accommodating, MBAs did have a reputation for looking out for number one. What did he want from her?

"Tell me, why that introductory speech on the terrace?"

He blushed.

"It was entertaining."

His eyes picked up some interior light. Then he pulled a silver flask from inside his coat and handed it to her.

"Here. Dutch courage, as they say. In this case, Conde de Osborne brandy. From Jerez. Careful, though, it goes down a bit too easily."

She took a swig of the silky liquor warmed by his body. The world, she decided, had another nipple. She handed back the flask.

"Comes in a bottle designed by Salvador Dalí."

"After drinking enough of it I imagine things look pretty surreal."

Instead of drinking, he tucked the bottle back in his jacket. "Anyway, I like to know something about where I'm living, and Spain is fascinating. So many contradictions and idiosyncrasies. And, well I wanted to impress you."

"Get us out of here and I'll definitely be impressed."

For a few moments they listened for any sound, but all around them remained quiet.

Michael continued. "Telephones work great, though. During the civil war generals would call up to the front to find out if they were winning or if they were supposed to surrender."

"So, were you a fascist or a Republican?"

"Fascist. It's mostly Republicans with speaking parts. Nat saved those for his cronies. But I can't complain. It's a paying job. Today was the last day though. Like I said, I'm dead now."

"You never know. They might need to reshoot." She paused for a moment, beginning to understand why he might want to impress her. "So you don't have a regular job."

"No. And I've been out of school nearly a year."

"How do you support yourself?"

"Investments," he said offhandedly. "But I'm not very good at being idle. At the same time, I don't want just anything. Though the money's not as good in Spain as other parts of Europe, I'd rather stay here. Maybe I'll be a movie star. Do you think I could be a movie star?"

"I haven't seen you act," she said carefully. "How did you come to live with Nathan?"

"School. We were in the same class."

"Are you friends?"

"When he gets me parts in movies," he said and laughed.

"What do you know about the director, Freddie Frazier?"

Michael shrugged. "Can't really tell you much. We extras take our orders from an assistant director. I've never even spoken to him."

"I just wanted to know how understanding he is. There's a bus leaving at noon and I'm supposed to be on it."

"Not much I can do. Everyone's at the school right now but I didn't see any coach, er, bus."

"How did Nathan come to be Frazier's personal assistant?"

Even in the dim light, she could see Michael's eyes darken. His eyes were most revealing of his thoughts. If he could manipulate that quality, he'd possess an essential element of good film acting.

"Nat's related to Carlos Ballester's wife," he said. "You know who he is?"

"At this point I'm a blank slate."

"Well, Carlos Ballester is responsible for the film's financing. He's one of the wealthiest men in Catalonia—or maybe I should say 'was.' He's connected with the business school and Opus Dei. Though he's not a professor, he's been a guest lecturer."

"You don't like him?"

He sat straighter. "I didn't say that!"

Your eyes did, she thought.

He laughed nervously. "Let's just say, he defines arrogance. I almost went to work for him until—"

The light came on and the elevator itself jerked slightly, then resumed its descent, effectively cutting off his sentence. They both grinned in relief and scrambled outside when the door slid open. Queenie decided it might be prudent to add Our Lady of Electricity to her pantheon of female deities.

"You speak Spanish?" Michael asked, as they walked to the front door.

"Barely. And you?"

"Of course. You'll find most Europeans speak at least two languages. I personally speak five: Dutch, English, Italian, German, and French."

He pushed the door open for her.

"With Spanish, that's six."

"I didn't say I could count."

"Business school must have been a real challenge," she

remarked. He laughed good-naturedly and led her to the familiar silver Jaguar parked on the sidewalk.

"Look, if you need a translator or a guide, Queenie, I'm available . . . and don't forget me when you're writing the script."

"I'll keep you in mind, Michael."

CHAPTER SEVEN

MICHAEL SLID THE Jag smoothly into a parking place on a quiet street. Barcelona's heavy and frenetic pace was only a distant roar here in Pedrables, a wealthy, manicured section of the city several miles south of the apartment. En route Michael had pointed out the local underground that would take her down to the Ramblas, the famous tree-lined promenade down by the harbor; the nearest tobacconist, where she could also buy stamps; several old churches; and a monastery. He also told her, with a disarming grin, that she could buy penicillin over the counter if she needed it. He then added that to show their high regard for Dr. Alexander Fleming, the discoverer of penicillin, most of the major cities of Spain had a street named after him. *Before* penicillin, Michael explained, bull-fighters who were gored had been more than likely to die of septic poisoning. She found the commentary interesting but what was Michael thinking? That she was more likely to run with the bulls or contract VD while in Spain?

They hurried along a high wall toward an open gate. Queenie anxiously looked around for a bus, but didn't see one. The time now being a little after twelve, she'd probably missed it.

"Look, if they left, I can always drive you to the location. I mean, I've got Frazier's car."

"Do you know where it is?"

"I can find out."

Upon entering the grounds of the business school, they followed a flagstone path between several contemporary-looking buildings. The grounds were terraced and richly land-scaped, with well-tended gardens. At the far edge of a wide central courtyard stood an elegant old cream-colored Span-ish building that appeared to have once been a residence. Ivy crept along one side and around tall arched doors, past a balcony and up to the terra-cotta tiled roof. Michael told her it housed a formal bar and well-appointed meeting rooms. She couldn't have cared less.

Passing this structure, they came to a wide lawn complete with a pond and sheltering trees. Michael led her down sev-eral levels toward another more modern building.

At the bottom of a flight of steps he paused. Through a solid wall of glass they could see into a room crowded with platoons of wounded soldiers. In the far left corner was a partitioned area where a couple of men were watching a video monitor. One of the men was Freddie Frazier. Relief made Queenie momentarily weak. Michael looked disap-pointed.

Then Queenie spied Nathan skirting the soldiers and com-ing to meet them at the door. He stood out in the contemporary uniform of T-shirt, jeans, and baseball cap, the latter sporting the familiar interlocking N and Y of the New York Yankees. There were so many reasons to despise this cretin.

"Nando's really pissed you weren't here at eight," Nathan greeted her.

Queenie tensed. "Whose fault is that?" she retorted.

But Nathan wasn't listening. "Keys, deBeers."

Michael handed them over, then smiled brightly at Queenie. "Call if you need me. I'm in the directory." Then he extended the typewriter. "Here. Almost forgot about this."

For a moment, as he shot a look at Michael, Nathan's eyes made her think of her white Persian's look whenever the cat was angry. She half expected Nathan to bare his teeth and hiss.

Michael joined some friends, and Nathan ushered Queenie toward the partition. "Be sure to call him *Señor* Frazier," Nathan instructed. "Why'd you bring the type-writer?"

"For balance," she snapped.

"The writer's finally here, Nando," Nathan said, obviously thinking he was introducing them. Then he slipped away.

"Glad you could finally make it, Miss Davilov," Freddie replied coolly. She couldn't tell if he was genuinely angry or if he was simply putting on a show for those who might be listening.

"Your personal assistant should learn how to tell time. I've been waiting since eight."

"There are plenty of cabs."

"No one told me where you'd be, *Señor* Frazier."

"Oh!" He seemed momentarily taken aback.

He moved to his chair. "Well then, why don't you get

something to drink. We'll talk after lunch. Nat'll show you to the kitchen."

She wanted to ask him about departing for the location, but that would give away foreknowledge. She'd have to wait for his cue.

Maybe he read her mind. "Uh, we'll be leaving for the location later—as soon as I can run down the bloody coach. Glad you thought to bring the typewriter."

She started to leave, then he said, "One more thing, Miss Davilov." His expression could only be described as long-suffering. "Call me Freddie. Not Señor Frazier. Not Nando. Just Freddie. Okay?"

"Sure."

Nat hovered on the other side of the partition. He'd obviously been eavesdropping.

"Stay away from me," she snapped, brushing past him.

"I'm supposed to show you where the kitchen is."

"I'll find it better without you."

If *People* magazine was to be believed, British actor Tybalt St. Germain was one of the "sexiest men alive." His parents had been minor thespians who named him after a prominent Capulet in Shakespeare's *Romeo and Juliet*, the play in which they met. Tybalt (pronounced "Tibul") began his career on the stage but his charismatic looks destined him for the big screen's greater audience. In the past fifteen years or so, he had been considered—if not first choice, definitely second—for the lead in many major Hollywood productions. But he was quirky, sometimes choosing lesser roles in British, Australian, and European films with smaller budgets. Quality, he stressed in interviews, keyed his choices.

"Actors should be remembered for their performances, not their bloody salaries," he had once vociferously declared after a late-night television host requested confirmation of a rather astronomical sum Tybalt was being paid for his role as Carlos, in a film that romanticized the infamous international terrorist. An instant later, Tybalt had stalked off the set and out of the television studio, leaving the host to rely on his wit. (They'd cut to commercial.)

And there were chunks of time during which he simply disappeared, and a year or two would pass before he even read a script let alone went before the cameras. But during those absences, rumor kept him firmly entrenched in the public psyche: alternately he was a British spy, a drunk with a penchant for yearlong binges, and a lothario who preferred illiterate women and had fathered children in the Australian outback, the jungles of New Guinea, the Siberian tundra, and even Tierra del Fuego.

If that wasn't silly enough, *Beyond Belief*, a British rag patterned after *News of the World*, had once declared that it had proof Tybalt had actually led the "Charge of the Light Brigade" and was well over a hundred and fifty years old. Perhaps someone simply confused him with the Comte de Saint-Germain, a mysterious Frenchman influential in the court of Louis XV, and purported to be at that time more than two thousand years old. The American tabloid *World Abuzz* had once announced that *Tybalt St. Germain* was an anagram for a warlord on the star Betelgeuse, a red giant in the constellation Orion. But while Tybalt's pulchritude may have seemed to some unearthly, he still had the standard consignment of universally accepted body parts and all in the normal places. The configuration, though, was more enviable than most.

His personal life reflected his career in its idiosyncrasies. At age nineteen, he'd been briefly married to Maggie Dawes, one of Britain's greatest stage actresses and twenty-five years his senior. Not only that, she was his godmother. The ink on the scandal sheets had barely dried when Ms. Dawes drowned in a boating accident, leaving Tybalt a very rich young man. He'd never remarried, but seemed to prefer liaisons with other men's wives.

Tybalt St. Germain also wrote cookbooks, all best-sellers. Was it culinary genius that allowed him to roll over Betty Crocker, as it were, or was it the photographs of him stirring stews or chopping veggies while wearing only a bibbed apron that rocketed sales? *Buns and Pastries*, his first, featured as many luscious edibles as shots of his backside. In any case, his books provided a lot to chew on.

He turned from what looked like an enormous flat-bottomed wok.

Feeling a little giddy over finding the star in the kitchen, Queenie took a moment to compose herself. He wore heavy boots and the familiar apron over grungy trousers and a string vest. At least he was dressed. She might have embarrassed herself had he not been.

"Hell-o," he said cheerfully. Both hands were busy arranging small mussels, still in the shell, around the sides of the pan. "Just in time. You can clean and chop the squid, thank you very much. Over there." He nodded toward a large stainless steel sink.

Queenie didn't immediately move which seemed to annoy him.

"*Habla inglés?*"

She cleared her throat. "Of course. I'm American."

He laughed; she couldn't figure out why. Then he said,

"Leave it to Freddie to find an *American* cook. Bloody hell. Well we're not preparing hamburgers, sweetheart."

"I'm not a cook."

The laughter abruptly stopped. He now regarded her with suspicion. "What are you doing here then? I don't like to be bothered while cooking."

"Uh, Freddie suggested I get something to drink and wait for him here."

"Who are you?"

"My name's Queenie Davilov."

"And?" he said impatiently, obviously seeing no need to introduce himself.

"And what?"

"—are you doing here?"

"I just told you," she replied testily. His sexy screen persona notwithstanding, communication didn't seem to be one of his strong points. Then in a more pleasant tone, she added, "I'll be glad to help while I'm waiting. But I'm better with vegetables. Last time I saw a squid was in *Twenty Thousand Leagues Under the Sea*."

He wiped his hands on his apron and moved briskly to the sink. She joined him.

"What I meant was, what's your purpose? You an actress?"

"Oh. Well, no. I'm the script doctor."

His brown eyes widened momentarily. "Ah. Andrew's description was well off the mark. You don't look the least bit like a troll."

"He said that about me?" she asked, astonished. Then the thought struck her that Tybalt might be pulling her leg.

"You must admit one's replacement is never very attractive. Poor chap rang me last night. Thought I could get his job back for him. . . . I hope you're not planning a long stay."

"Just show me how to clean these suckers—thank you very much," she snapped.

While he may have been trying to tease a reaction out of her, it was she who got the reaction out of him. For a moment, his jaw locked in anger and his eyes gave off little sparks.

Her encounters since leaving L.A. suggested the gathering of unpredictable and temperamental forces. She considered spitting, a trick she'd learned in a meditation class to ward off anger, but while it worked on the streets of L.A. she didn't think it would be a good idea here in the kitchen.

Then, instead of instructing her in the art of preparing squid, Tybalt strode to the back corner of the kitchen, where a small table and two wooden chairs were set up. A frayed jacket hung on the back of a chair along with a large leather bag. When he turned around, she saw him unsheathe a foot-long bayonet with a gradually curved blade about a foot long.

Any doubt about the seriousness with which he took his cooking instantly vanished. Queenie considered a swift exit, then decided to hold her ground. She had to work with this man, should she survive, and she was determined not to let him intimidate her. But instead of threatening her, he crossed to the large institutional refrigerator and removed a bottle of chilled champagne. She watched, now fascinated, reminding herself that even offscreen, actors were likely to give performances. Whether this one was good or bad remained to be seen.

He twisted the wire off the cork, then aimed the bottle just above her head. Gently, he ran the blade along the bottle neck, then with a sudden swift stroke the bayonet connected with the cork, shooting it into a corner of the ceiling. A froth spilled over and he quickly poured himself a glass. He drank it down, and immediately refilled it. He smiled. She knew he'd enjoyed the performance, especially her discomfort when he pulled out the bayonet.

"Not exactly Excalibur," he remarked, holding the blade erect by its beveled pommel while twisting it back and forth. "Crimean War, actually."

"Are you going to relate your experiences at the Battle of Balaklava?" she said, trying to keep a straight face.

"You read *Beyond Belief*, do you?"

"For its hysterical rather than historical content."

"Actually, this belonged to a distant relation," he said, striking a blow to the fanciful. "I use it for more cultural pursuits—like opening bottles of champagne. Maybe you *don't* know that I will not cook if I'm in a foul mood—being a great believer in the power of negative energy. It can ruin a meal. Let's hope the champagne quickly reinstates my good humor."

He sheathed the bayonet and returned to the sink with the bottle. "I'd offer you some but, being a writer, you'd probably accept. Besides, you'll need both hands."

"And what if I'm in a foul mood?"

He took a step back. His attitude abruptly changed, as if he were seeing her for the first time as a person. After a beat he spoke. "Well then—what did you say your name is?"

"Queenie Davilov."

"Hmm. Can't say I like it much. But neither do I like my own. . . . Yes, well, we must get you a glass."

In this film family, drinking seemed to be as much a part of life as breathing. She'd have to learn, and quickly, to pace herself.

"Tell me about the script," she said. "Who are you playing?"

"Let's leave that to Freddie, shall we?"

For a few minutes they talked about cooking and found their common ingredient, as it were, to be the stinking rose. She told him about the annual garlic festival in Gilroy, California, where she'd eaten garlic ice cream and drunk garlic wine. He expressed an interest in going sometime. And would cause a riot, she mused.

"Have you read any of my cookbooks?" he asked while topping off their glasses, and actually seemed a little shy, as if her answer was important.

"I had them all. My favorite was *I Love You Stew*. Honestly, I liked them as much for the recipes and commentary as the pictures."

"What'd you do, give them away? Sell them?"

"Oh no, lost them in the January quake."

"Bloody hell! How'd you make out?"

"I managed to save my computer and the kitty. The clothes weren't important. I've picked up a few things at secondhand stores. Losing my library and artwork was painful. Not to mention the films I'd made in college—and some awards for films I'd worked on."

She thought of but didn't mention the old .45 Smith and Wesson that had been given to her by her former boss, the late I. P. Friedman. She'd carried it a few times during her work as a private investigator, but had never fired it. The gun hadn't been too big for her hand but was a tad heavy. She could well have landed on her ass from the recoil. Still, she regretted the loss. For sentimental reasons.

"Fortunately, my best scripts were on the hard disk. We were all angry when the authorities condemned the building and wouldn't allow us back in. My boyfriend lost everything that wasn't parked on the street or in a deposit box." She drained her glass. "But at times like that, what you have means more than what you've lost. People died, after all."

"You did find a place to live?"

"I've been staying with a friend. It's hard. Seems like everyone in L.A.'s looking for a place."

"At least you have experience surviving disasters. Should come in handy."

"What do you mean?"

"We've had our share on this film. I imagine you've heard of our disappearing writer. Just before that a whole load of equipment went plummeting down a ravine. Massive explosion. The driver was having drinks at the time. But lorries don't drive themselves. But, enough of that." He nodded toward the dining room. "That lot out there must be getting acquainted with hunger, though I daresay, from the sound, they've broken into the wine."

He put his glass down and picked up one of the pale squids. "Are you feeling positive?"

"Positively."

He gave her a sensual smile. "Are you married?"

"No."

For a moment she thought she saw disappointment. Then he got down to business. "Right. Now, grasp the body in one hand. With the other, pull out the unfortunate creature's *tent*acles . . ."

Drinking champagne, discussing garlic, and dismembering cephalopods with one of the world's sexual icons, she thought. *Holy Mother.*

CHAPTER EIGHT

USING GREAT WADS of white cotton towels, Queenie helped carry the heavy paella pans—clusters of them had been hidden until now in ovens—into the dining hall, which smelled more like a lockerroom than an eatery. No one seemed to mind as they shoveled mounds of the saffron- and seafood-scented rice onto white plates. Michael caught her eye as he poured wine, a bottle of red in his left hand, white in his right, for his fellows. Whether he poured by choice or direction she didn't know. However, he performed the task with good humor, making comments in an assortment of languages.

Perspiring from exertion and the heat from the open ovens, Queenie finally sank into one of the chairs in the kitchen and poured a glass from a freshly uncorked bottle. She stared at Tybalt's jacket hanging on the empty chair opposite her.

Her brain felt like grits, a grainy half-cooked mixture of jet lag, fatigue, anxiety, sweat, and champagne.

"Good lass," Tybalt declared, dropping a pan on a burner. "Christ, I'm knackered. Did you have some?"

She shook her head.

"Have a feed, love. Made yourself more useful than most writers."

She sipped champagne, her eyes neither blinking nor wavering from the jacket, her brain barely registering the clatter of plates, the bursts of laughter, and the drone of conversation from the other room. Once Tybalt had opened all the oven doors, the kitchen had become stifling.

Tybalt dropped into the chair, breaking her link with his jacket. She looked up at his face. Far from "knackered," he looked ready for anything. He poured more champagne and smiled. "Bloody hell, you sweat like a man."

She didn't answer.

"I like that in a woman." He raised his glass. "Cheers." Then he lit a cigarette.

Her *third* job—as a kitchen grunt—aside, she remembered her second—or was it the first?

"Tybalt, what do you think happened to Digby Patterson?"

He turned away, blowing smoke into the hot kitchen mist. "Haven't a clue. But that shouldn't bother you, seeing as how you've got his job."

"I can't help but be curious," she said, adding lightly, "maybe it's common to screenwriters in Spain."

"Didn't happen to Andrew."

"In a sense, it did."

"Hmm. Yes, I see your point."

"When did you last see Mr. Patterson?"

He glanced toward the ceiling. "Last Friday night, it was.

At the location. We shared a few pints at the local pub." He stopped and drank some champagne.

"Did you get the feeling he was planning to take a hike?"

Tybalt eyed her suspiciously. "You sound positively Holmesian. Not a detective are you?"

She wondered if Andrew had told Tybalt about Carmella's prognostications, specifically that she was a spy. "Look, if he shows up, I'm out of a job. I just want to know what my chances are."

"Nothing against you, but I hope he pops in. Digs always consults actors, likes their input, especially with dialogue," he said. "Sometimes, you know, it seems as if one has, rather than words, a mouth full of porridge. Not to worry, though. Freddie can always keep you on as kitchen help. Now I must go see where the cleanup crew's gone off to."

Once he had left, Queenie put her head down, thinking she'd take a short nap. Her eyelids quivered. Porridge, she thought. *Grits.*

She awoke with a start and checked her watch. Three thirty. Abruptly, she grabbed the satchel and stood up. Tybalt and his jacket were gone. She hurried into the dining hall. No one was there.

Outside, clouds covered the sun. The heat she'd felt earlier had dissipated. Now her skin felt cold and clammy. She found a coffee urn and helped herself to a cup of its syrupy contents. At least the coffee was hot. She drank it down and warmed her hands around a second cup, reminding herself that spring weather was not to be trusted.

Surveying the tables littered with the remains of lunch, she wondered if someone expected her to clean up.

"No way, José," she snapped, miffed at this latest annoyance. She plopped down in front of a half-eaten plate of food and rolled a cigarette. For a moment she considered taking a taxi back to the airport. Maybe Eric, confused by thirty-dollar hot dogs, champagne, and too many screenings, had made a terrific mistake. She lit the cigarette.

Then she remembered the video monitor.

Moving around the partition, she sat in Freddie's chair, beside which were two metal cases filled with videocassettes, each labeled with the film's title, location, and scene numbers, some with the notation "edited/sound." She felt a spurt of excitement. She didn't have a script, no one had told her the story, but she had some elementary footage. Nor did it much matter that it was probably out of sequence; she'd worked as a script supervisor on three films and knew quite well how to piece together fragments of a story.

Saying a prayer to Our Lady of Electricity, she checked to see that the power was on then slipped a cassette into the VCR. And there on the screen was her neighbor.

CHAPTER NINE

FASCINATED, QUEENIE WATCHED the woman, not in bathrobe and curlers but wearing an elegant evening gown circa the late 1930s, her earlobes and neck studded with diamonds. She was dancing on a terrace with a boy of ten or eleven. They moved gracefully through pools of light from tall arched windows through which a party could be seen in a high-ceilinged room. The woman and boy danced alternately in shadow and light.

An older man appeared. "Carlos. Time for bed."

"Oh, let us finish our dance," the woman protested in heavily accented English.

"He's had enough for tonight and you, my dear, have not met all of our guests."

The woman kissed the boy on the cheek. "Do as your father says. There's a good boy."

"Good night, mama," the boy said stiffly.

The boy exited through a doorway; seemed to merge with the blazing light, then disappeared.

"Oh Miguel, these people are so dull. All they talk about is the coming war."

"Hush, Cristiana! Besides, there's an English journalist just arrived you might find amusing."

In another series of scenes, Queenie watched the character, Cristiana, in a dove-gray dress tossing evening gowns out of a massive armoire, then gathering them all and dropping them over a balustrade to the floor below. In another scene, she went from room to room, stripping beds of their linen.

On another tape, Cristiana, the boy, and a blonde in her mid-thirties sat together cutting up the clothing and linens, backlighted by the glow of a hearth fire. The sound of their scissors provided background noise.

"All these beautiful clothes. Such a waste!" said the blond woman.

"Be sure to cut out all the labels, Carlos."

The blond woman smiled wryly. "You think a wounded soldier would refuse a bandage if he knew it came from a Berlin dress shop?"

"Miguel said I'm suspected of being a fascist collaborator! Can you imagine anything so ridiculous?"

For a moment the blond woman looked worried. Then she whispered, "Well, just tell everyone who your lover is. That should settle any doubt."

"Hannah!" Cristiana said with a laugh.

And this scene on another cassette:

Hannah and Cristiana are traveling along Balmes when the car is stopped. On a wall behind them, the Disney character the Big Bad Wolf looks out cunningly. FASCISMO! is scrawled beneath him. Further down, Popeye's punch sends

Mussolini reeling. A man orders the two women out of the car at gunpoint.

"Papers!" he demands.

Annoyed, Cristiana takes papers from her handbag. While he peruses them, she says: "We are taking bandages to the hospital. How do you expect us to get there if we're stopped every few blocks?"

"Get out of the car."

Another man rifles through the sacks.

"Guns are being smuggled to fascist sympathizers, Señora Ballester. I see your maid is German."

"And so am I, Señor. We have lived in Barcelona since I was a child. Neither of us are any more fascist than the Mediterranean!"

"I'm afraid we'll have to detain her. You go on. Take the bandages to the hospital."

Looking worried, Cristiana turns to Hannah. "I'll ring Miguel. He'll take care of everything."

Hannah appears defiant. "Don't worry about me."

And in another scene:

Cristiana is packing a suitcase with Carlos's clothes. Miguel enters.

"What are you doing, Cristiana?"

"I'm taking Carlos to the country. The city is no place for him now."

"The country is worse. Don't you pay attention? They're bombing villages."

"Anzana isn't even on the map."

Miguel grabs her by the wrist. "You will not take my son from this house."

Gently, Cristiana removes his hand. "Miguel, listen to me. I can protect him far better than you. You're always gone on business. We're too vulnerable here. Please, let me take him to safety."

"Barcelona will never fall!"

"Catalan pride won't stop Franco. Be reasonable. It's only a matter of time."

Miguel regards her angrily. "That British journalist has put silly thoughts in your head. He's a Communist, isn't he?"

"Better than a fascist."

"Not to be trusted. Now unpack."

She begins putting clothes back into the wardrobe. When he is gone, she leans wearily against the wardrobe and looks down at her slightly swollen belly.

After several tense domestic scenes, Queenie watched as:

Cristiana syphons gasoline from a car while Hannah keeps a nervous watch.

The scene cuts to Cristiana, carrying a basket and leading a sleepy Carlos to a car. He climbs in the backseat and crawls under a blanket. Hannah tosses a suitcase in the trunk on top of bundles of rags. The barrel of a gun peeks out. Hannah covers it, then quietly closes the trunk and begins to push. Cristiana steers the car out of the garage. The engine engages.

Panting, Hannah jumps into the passenger seat. "Miguel's going to be furious—"

"He knows we'll be safer in the country," Cristiana snaps.

"—that you stole his petrol!"

Another cassette began with the camera angled on a stark, leafless tree, snowy mountains in the background. The deep quiet was suddenly pierced by the sound of three gunshots. The camera held on the tree a moment, after which could be heard the crescendoing sound of footsteps crunching through the snow. The camera lowered to four men with weathered faces wearing black berets. They wore dark, worn clothing and carried a pine coffin. They entered a small graveyard with less than a dozen white crosses.

A civil guard in a fresh uniform and distinctive hat, the black patent leather *tricornio*, stood to one side while they lowered the coffin into a fresh grave. The last shot was a close-up of a wooden cross on which was crudely carved along the traverse plank CRISTIANA KAUFMANN BALLESTER. Above and below on the upright were the dates 1910 and 1938, respectively.

As the next scene began to roll, Freddie and Tybalt appeared in the room. Queenie shut off the VCR.

"Good," Freddie said. "I'm glad you've acquainted yourself with the film. I'll arrange a proper screening later."

Freddie rewound the tape. "There's been a problem with the coach. Seems this morning the Opus Dei wives took it to Torreciudád in Aragon. We've been trying to track down another." He removed the tape from the VCR. "Without any luck. They're expected at five." He glanced at the littered tables. "Any sign of the cleaning staff?"

"I haven't seen anyone," Queenie said.

"C'mon luv," Tybalt said with a smile. "Help me with the washing up?" Of all the things he was or might be, St. Germain couldn't be accused of being a fussy prima donna.

"One moment, Queenie," Freddie said. While Tybalt began stacking plates, Freddie brought out from a folio papers which she first mistook for the script. There were hardly enough pages. A treatment, maybe?

"Your contract."

"Oh."

"I need you to read and sign."

Standard fare—there were no surprises good or bad, payment was assessed per diem and for a period not to exceed (in this case) ten days. As up-front money, the equivalent of five days had already been paid.

Freddie told her he'd given Eric the check. She figured her check, less Eric's ten percent, was on its way to her mail drop in West Hollywood. Having no fixed address at the moment, she'd availed herself of the service.

After both of them signed two copies, one for her and one for him, she felt a little relieved. A *little*. Generally, film contracts were like stop signs—often they simply slowed people rather than stopping them completely. And in Hollywood anyway, lawsuits were such an integral part of the business that they weren't always hostile. Queenie imagined the jargon might evolve into a friendly, "Let's do court."

So, while Freddie packed the video equipment, Queenie helped Tybalt clean up the dining room and load the industrial washer.

Never say "No way, José," she thought ruefully.

At around five thirty, the cast and a skeleton crew waited outside the school grounds for the bus, which, they'd just learned, had been waiting at Sants train station for *them* but was now on its way. Freddie was busy down the street checking out the equipment truck. The cameras and video equipment were carefully packed in the Jaguar, which Nathan would drive.

When the female lead stepped out of a taxi a little after five, Queenie had introduced herself.

"You're playing Cristiana," she'd said. "We sort of met

this morning when I interrupted you. I'm Queenie Davilov."

The woman frowned.

"This morning. On the terrace."

"Ah, now I recognize you. I am Nuria Escola. Uh, my English is very bad when upset." She was not a beauty, certainly not in the Hollywood tradition. Her eyes were too close together, her nose too lumpy, but there was a bone-deep determination about her that translated to a certain strength Queenie saw both in person and on the small screen.

"Well, Nuria, I've seen tapes of the dailies. Your English is excellent."

Nuria's eyes immediately brightened. Actors have an extra organ that is nourished by honest compliments. Feed that organ and you've gained an ally. Even nutrient-deficient flattery will get you close.

"On the terrace I practice English with bad, um, accent. My dialogue coach say to exaggerate first. You, uh, are Andrew's girlfriend?"

"Hardly. I'm his replacement."

Nuria considered this for a moment. She looked around then moved closer, speaking softly. "Be careful. You know Nathan?"

"He picked me up at the airport."

"Before Andrew was Digby—a great writer! My bedroom is by the elevator. I hear it and go to the door thinking maybe my, uh, friend comes to visit me. Then I see Nathan go into the apartment. Very late he does this. When Digby sleeping." Then Nuria's attention was drawn to a cab pulling up. A woman stepped out.

"Oh! My dialogue coach." Just before moving away, she whispered, "Keep both eyes on Nathan."

As if one eye would stray when Nathan came in sight.

Around six, the bus pulled up and the driver got out—and kept going. Freddie chased after him and, after a brief confrontation, Freddie returned. "Anyone here with experience driving a coach?"

In answer, there were numerous groans. Freddie held up his hands. "Only joking. A new driver's on his way. Go ahead and board."

Queenie took a window seat in the center, wondering if this was another example of Murphy's Law—or had someone deliberately stalled the trip?

Nathan and Freddie loaded provisions, which included food and enough wine to keep everyone happily unaware of any further annoyances. Nuria and her dialogue coach took seats in front of Queenie. Tybalt suggested that they watch the dailies while waiting, and fiddled with a TV monitor secured to the ceiling at the front of the bus. But there was no VCR in which to insert a tape and he finally gave up. Apparently it wouldn't work unless the engine was engaged. Meanwhile, Queenie thought it wise to locate the emergency exits.

Around six thirty the driver arrived, greeted by a hearty round of applause. A few moments later the bus pulled out followed by the equipment truck and Nathan bringing up the rear in the Jaguar.

Now there was only one problem.

CHAPTER TEN

LIKE A PAPAL edict, Pope John Paul II's earnest, rosy-cheeked face beamed from the TV monitor. In Spanish and at full volume he directed his captive audience in the art of being a good Catholic wife.

The broadcast began when the bus started up. Tybalt and Freddie swayed in the aisle trying unsuccessfully to turn the machine off. Both men's curses competed with the Pope's more gentle message.

Nuria sat with her back to the window and translated for Queenie. Apparently, they needed a remote control device, and finally decided that the first driver had taken it with him.

"The situation," Nuria said, both amused and proud, "is very Spanish." She made an expansive gesture, sloshing wine on her seatmate.

"Dammit! Nuria, look what you've done."

"*Eh mujer! Muy tranquil!*"

Vexed, the woman went to the bathroom in the back.

Unfazed, Nuria went on. "Now the pope is talking about sex. What do you suppose *he* knows about it? Bah! Priests telling women what to do. Is *ridiculoso,* no?" She watched the monitor for a moment then turned back to Queenie.

"Now he talks about the evil of abortion." Her face darkened for a moment. "You know Cristiana, my character?"

"Yes," Queenie replied.

"A great woman. Very strong." Nuria sipped her wine, wiping some from her chin. "What if she try to have an abortion? Can you imagine what that is like? In España!"

"You mean, when she was pregnant with Carlos?"

"Oh no! The second time." She opened her arms. "You and me, all of us, would not be here."

"Why?"

Before Nuria could answer, Freddie called for attention. Tybalt took a seat.

In a half shout, Freddie said, "It seems that God, or someone, has decided that the pope accompany us on our journey. Regretfully, we are unable to shut off the bloody machine. So, we shall simply carry on. I'm sorry but all things considered, we could have worse company."

The dialogue coach returned, the front of her white blouse damp but wine-free. She barked at Nuria to sit properly, then the two began rehearsing.

Freddie balanced himself on the dialogue coach's seat back and spoke to Queenie. "Sorry, I'd planned to introduce you but it'll keep till later."

"How long a trip is it?"

"We should be there in about an hour and a half." She

noted that he didn't speak in absolute certainties. "Would you like some wine?"

"Is there coffee?"

"Afraid not."

A moment later he returned with a bottle and two cups and began speaking as if they were continuing an interrupted conversation. She wondered if he was losing his mind.

"Frankly, I find the thought of European homogeneity appalling. Diversity not only offers cultural enrichment, it blocks certain political control. I fear the so-called economic stability envisioned by the EEC. It stinks of an eventual dictatorship."

"That seems to be a leap."

He lit a cigarette. "History is recorded in leaps. And from Caesar onward, European history reads like a series of one-man shows." He sighed. "At least England should remain relatively safe. Graced by the benevolence of geography, England can survive anything—except maybe the prevailing winds from Madison Avenue."

Sitting stiffly in his seat, he smoked in silence for a moment.

"Why don't you take a nap?" Queenie suggested gently.

He glanced over and gave her a rare, quick smile. "My dear, I'm wired for the duration. A proper sleep would ruin me." He suddenly perked. "Eric mentioned a book you'd written about the Spanish civil war."

Queenie felt her face go hot. "Actually, it was a film I made. About Dolores Ibarruri, la Pasionaria."

"Fascinating! Did you bring it?"

"I lost it in the earthquake."

"Dear God! That must have been horrific. Did you lose much?"

"Let's just say I now try to avoid strong attachments to material things."

"But you know, I find it easier to work with people who have a disaster or two under their belts. . . . Now then, having seen some of the footage, what do you think? Mind you, once we've settled in, I'll arrange for a proper screening."

"Well . . . Nuria's quite good—but I really didn't see enough to form an opinion. Can't you just give me the story line, tell me what you want me to do?"

"Actually, I find it most difficult to encapsulate a project in a few sentences. You see, I tend to see everything at once—which is why I'm not a writer. So please, you ask and I'll answer."

Queenie sipped her wine, taking a moment to order her thoughts. "Okay, well, to begin I'm curious about this Spanish-British link. A major British star, a Spanish unknown playing the lead? And why does a British director want to make a film not only about the Spanish civil war—at the heart of which was a tremendous class struggle—but a *privileged* Spanish woman? I'm assuming it is about her, since she seemed to be the focal point in the few scenes I saw."

Freddie stubbed out his cigarette in the armrest's ashtray. "Eric didn't tell you?"

Queenie laughed, then lowering her voice said, "As I mentioned earlier, Eric wasn't long on details."

He topped off his wine, careful to anticipate the movement of the bus. "Right. Actually, I don't remember if I said much about the story to him myself.

"Anyway, it all comes together in one simple fact," he said and placed the bottle between his legs. "Cristiana, you see, was my mother."

CHAPTER ELEVEN

QUEENIE STARED THOUGHTFULLY at the nubbed fabric of the seat in front of her. She could hear Nuria reciting in English, changing *donut* to *do not*. Was it Andrew who had told her her Spanish would improve with wine? Whatever— the beverage seemed to help Nuria shape her words. Then she remembered Nuria's speech on the terrace:

"Ian . . . he'll know it's not . . . his."

Queenie put that together with the party scene she'd viewed on the video monitor, and Nuria's comments about an abortion, and suddenly knew who Tybalt St. Germain had been cast to play.

"And your father was the journalist Cristiana's husband mentioned in the scene on the terrace? Ian?" Queenie said.

"Well done! Yes, journalist and poet."

"Where are they?"

"Both dead. My father was killed by a sniper on the Ramblas and my mother was executed a month after I was born."

Queenie felt a slight tug on her guts followed by a moment of breathlessness. The reaction told her this was a good story. A *very* good story.

"To fill in the background," Freddie began, "Cristiana was German, from a very wealthy family with investments in Catalunya, in textile mills and factories, and a summer home in the foothills of the Catalunyan Pyrenees. During the First World War, they arranged for Cristiana and Hannah, her governess, to stay with friends in Barcelona. When her parents and older brother were killed in the war, Don Miguel Ballester, a close personal friend and business associate, became her guardian. And when she left school at sixteen, they married. At seventeen, she had a son, Carlos."

"Miguel was quite a bit older?" Queenie remembered the handsome actor who'd interrupted the dance on the terrace.

"Quite. In the film, he's a secondary character, little more than a cypher, really. In fact, we've finished shooting his scenes."

"So the story is about Cristiana and Ian?"

"And how they managed to have an affair given the barriers. It was extremely difficult for a highly visible, bourgeois *married* woman in a Catholic country to carry on with an equally visible foreigner, and during such extraordinary times. To complicate matters, being German-born, she automatically aroused suspicion. Remember, Barcelona was a Republican-anarchist stronghold. Many people believed she was a fascist sympathizer simply because of her birth. The situation for my father was almost as bad. Though he professed to be neutral, still, he'd written for Communist dailies before the war."

"Better a Communist than a fascist."

Freddie shook his head. "There were plenty of people who distrusted the Communists, especially when it became clear Stalin had betrayed them—that it was never his intention to supply badly needed aid. There might have been a considerably different outcome to the war had Stalin given more than lip service."

"I remember getting dizzy just trying to put all the factions together."

"For the sake of simplicity, let's say Spain was a pie unequally divided between the Nationalists, Communists, Republicans, fascists, and a few other misbegotten sorts, each piece wanting control of the whole."

He paused to drink his wine and light another cigarette. Queenie glanced out the window, where the twilight deepened into dark countryside. They were headed north on a highway with lots of space and few towns and villages in between. She became aware again of the pope, whom she had quite forgotten while Freddie told the story.

"Not all Nationalists were fascists, just as not all Communists or Republicans were anarchists."

"What about you?" Queenie asked. "How did you end up in England?"

"I lived under Don Miguel's roof until I was seven, though he made it clear, very early on, that he was not my father. After the war—World War II, that is—he located my father's family in Surrey. One day he told me I would be happier in England, that he had done his duty by caring for me until the war was over.

"Hannah, who'd been my mother's personal maid and who cared for me since my birth, took me to Madrid by train. We stayed there several days while she arranged for an *aya*, a governess, to travel and then live with me in England. By then, Hannah had married and couldn't go, but thought the transition would be easier if someone Spanish looked after me. It was quite a relief, as I spoke no English.

"Anyway, my governess was a rather wonderful person, quite beautiful. Like so many survivors, she'd lost her entire family during the civil war. Her name was Maria. My new family anglicized her name to Mary and mine to Freddie. I was quite lucky, actually, going from one wealthy household to another."

He drank some wine, his expression melancholy. "But for Mary, I believe I would have been a most unhappy child. My grandparents, well, were certainly kind. But as with Don Miguel, they weren't altogether receptive to a bastard child . . . and a Catholic one to boot."

Queenie's heart fluttered but she didn't interrupt.

"They pretty much left Mary and me to our own devices, installed us in a London townhouse. We spent most of our free time at the cinema. She was quite a fanatic, and, of course, I became one too. After the films we'd have tea and biscuits and discuss what we'd seen."

He reflected a moment, then said, "She had the most wonderful blond hair. Bleached, of course, which I didn't know until many years later. Funny I should think of her hair," he added absently.

"Is her character included in the film?"

"Oh no. She didn't come along until seven years after Cristiana's death. Anyway, we both became completely anglicized. She thought it best that I forget Spain. Sad memories, I suppose. I can barely speak the language anymore—just enough to get by . . . oh dear."

The bus began to slow and the driver yelled something.

"What now?" Freddie said and excused himself. Queenie

saw him make his way to the front, where he and the driver engaged in a loud discussion.

After a few minutes, Freddie returned, clearly relieved. "Just confirming the turnoff."

"Where is it we're going?"

"A restored convent, what's called a parador. It's quite small really, compared to some, but boasts indoor plumbing, comfortable beds, and one of the region's finest cooks. Nearby is the location where we'll be shooting—an abandoned village I purchased about fifteen years ago, for what amounts to around five thousand U.S. dollars."

"You own a whole village?"

"If you'd seen it then, you'd have thought I'd overpaid. It came with a population of stray burros, feral goats, wild pigs, and fleas. My God, the fleas! It's the village where Cristiana died. The inhabitants were massacred during reprisals after the war." He leaned into the aisle, looking nervously toward the front of the bus.

"I'd better make certain . . ." He left his seat.

After several miles, the driver pulled off the highway and onto a secondary road causing the bus to rock slightly. They'd entered the mountains and were now traveling dark, winding roads, ascending with each slow turn.

"So making this film hasn't been a spur of the moment affair," Queenie commented when Freddie settled back down.

"Not at all. One thing or another kept it from being a feasible project. Just as well, really, I was neither emotionally nor intellectually ready. It's odd how everything came together, what, six months ago? I ran into Digs at a party in London. He'd just gotten another divorce and I was in the market for a writer. Everything clicked. Two weeks later, he moved to Barcelona and began his research—not that simple for someone who doesn't speak the language."

"Did he stay at the apartment?"

"Oh no. The flat didn't become available until we secured financing. He found cheap digs in the Barrio Gótico—rather a rough though colorful part of the city just off the Ramblas.

"Trouble is, he's left me with no resolution."

"The burial scene I saw doesn't end the film?"

"Not quite. What I need requires the solution to one rather provocative mystery."

"That being?"

For a moment, he stared past her into the darkness. Then he turned slightly, the overhead light carving shadows on his bony face, making his eyes appear like dark hollows.

"She was executed, you see, taken into the woods and shot," he said faintly.

Neither Queenie nor Freddie spoke for a long minute while the bus swayed along the road, taking the narrow curves at too fast a clip—or so Queenie thought.

"And you want to know who pulled the trigger?"

As if he hadn't heard her, Freddie continued, his voice stronger. "Each village, you see, had a *cacique*, or political boss. They'd been around since well before the war. Their affiliations were known to change like the weather. This particular bloke allegedly did the deed. But before anything as extreme as execution could occur, two pieces of evidence had to be submitted against the accused.

"So, you see, the question is who presented the evidence against her? And what in God's name was it? It's possibly irrational of me, but I can't help but feel that there was some subtle treachery afoot. I believe *she* was betrayed."

CHAPTER TWELVE

ONE YELLOW LIGHT shone weakly above an arched portico. A wide veranda ran the length of the whitewashed parador, where clusters of rattan chairs and tables were set for guests to enjoy the eastern view. At the moment, the countryside spread like a black carpet to a sprinkling of lights tacked on the far edge.

Queenie stood apart from the activity. The *portero*, a wiry little man wearing a bright blue thigh-length cotton jacket and a black beret, helped the driver unload luggage while cast and crew members collected keys to their rooms. Freddie rushed back down the road nervously looking for the equipment truck and Nathan.

High beams suddenly shot toward the sky. A moment later, the truck appeared, with Freddie running alongside. He shouted to the driver and the truck was parked at the far end of the graveled lot. Then Nathan, behind the wheel of the silver Jaguar, cruised up the slope and parked behind the bus.

Freddie joined Queenie, briefly taking in the view while, hands on his hips, he caught his breath.

"The Costa Brava," he said, indicating the far lights. "Used to be quite the place." He glanced over his shoulder and called out to Nat.

Queenie turned and saw Nat stop just outside the entrance to the parador.

"Help me with the equipment."

"I need to get my room key."

"That can wait."

Sullenly, Nat plodded back to the Jag.

Freddie lowered his voice and said, "You're to have Digs's old room. Nathan wants it. Just go on and get the key from Señora Pujol. We'll meet in the dining room for supper."

Freddie then joined Nathan, and both men began unloading the camera equipment.

Queenie went into the parador, struck by a new consideration: What if Digby Patterson suddenly reappeared? If he did, would her services as an investigator be needed? Whatever other disasters had occurred, she figured Patterson's disappearance had been the catalyst to bring a P.I. on board.

Later, after a common Catalan meal of white beans and *butifarra* sausage, crusty bread, and a wonderful duck-liver pâté covered in crushed pepper, Queenie settled on the tiny balcony outside her room for a smoke.

Freddie had brought a copy of the script to her room before he and some of the others wandered down to the local tavern, as much to stretch their legs as to renew acquaintances with those villagers enlisted as extras in the film. They would be shooting at first light; after lunch tomorrow,

Freddie and Queenie would go over the script. That gave her time for a read. The story was so dramatic, so full of heroism, love, betrayal, and death, that it still somehow seemed alive and present. Enough mystery surrounded the story's conclusion that Digs's disappearance sounded a strange echo, and she wondered if there was some hidden logic connecting the script with the reason its author was missing.

Right now, though, she desired a few minutes to herself.

She could understand why Nathan might want this, a corner room, with both northern and eastern exposures. From what she'd seen, it was twice the size of the other rooms on the second floor, and even had a small fireplace.

The room was furnished with a canopied double bed, an antique armoire, and a writing desk and chair. Sheepskin rugs covered the stone floor. And unlike most of the other rooms, this one had a private bath complete with a claw-legged porcelain tub. As in the Barcelona apartment, there was a bidet and the toilet had a water tank mounted on the wall with a pull chain to flush. However, the wide laundry chute, probably once the privy and now covered by a faded tapestry, made her uneasy. It could be the draft that the tapestry failed to completely shut out. But anyone with an imagination could envision human-size creatures crawling up the shaft in the dead of night.

While she was glad of its size, she found the room gloomy; the lamp on the nightstand was unable to penetrate the shadowy corners. Further, when she asked Freddie why there was no phone in her room, she learned the only one was in the lobby. And all calls had to be logged.

For a moment, she reviewed the supper conversation. Someone, she couldn't recall who, had brought up the subject of Digby Patterson. This being Friday night, he'd been gone a week. Speculation about his whereabouts followed: He was shacked up with a Pyrenean shepherdess; he had gotten lost exploring one of the local caves; he'd been spirited away by Gypsies; he'd been eaten by wolves.

She did glean a couple of facts from the discussion. Digby Patterson had last been seen entering this room before midnight the previous Friday. This confirmed what Tybalt had told her in the school kitchen. Which meant someone had lost no time hiring another writer. Andrew had been on the job four days, Queenie one. So, the second day of Patterson's absence, the call had gone out to Andrew's agent and Andrew had immediately left Malta. Such quick action made Queenie wonder if someone had a good idea Digby wouldn't be returning. Freddie said he'd brought Andrew on board. Had he taken action himself or been advised to do so?

Further, if foul play wasn't involved, had Patterson simply walked away in the dead of night? And what happened to his belongings and his notes? Had he slid down the chute in the bathroom to avoid seeing anyone? If so, it was certainly odd behavior for a respected professional.

While rolling another cigarette she began to relax, not just for the first time since her arrival, but for the first time in months. Briefly, she considered her domestic situation.

The January quake had shot her out of her Hollywood residence of five years and into another zip code. Not that she minded leaving the rough neighborhood; it was the abruptness of her departure and the subsequent dependence on friends—Josephine Werlanda Burroughs, in particular. Joey, as she was commonly known, had given Queenie and her cat, Clue, a room in the house where Joey was house-sitting. Impermanence suited Joey but not Queenie. She needed a place of her own.

She lit the cigarette and inhaled deeply. This was no time to brood over mundane domestic issues, which, in any case, would wait until her return. More importantly, she needed a clearer picture of Digby Patterson, one sharply detailed. That required reflection.

A feral scent mingled with the sharp, refreshing smell of pine. She closed her eyes and took in the rich pheromones of nocturnal spring. Then she let herself drift back six years to her one and only encounter with the missing writer . . .

Crouching slightly, Queenie moved to the nearby door and left the conference room where, she was certain, her parting went unnoticed by the hundred-plus attendees. Visibly relieved, she made her way to the small bar and a cluster of umbrellaed tables set up in the otherwise empty rotunda of this older hotel located on Hollywood Boulevard.

The fee she'd paid to listen to prominent screenwriters and directors had been spent in vain. About all she'd learned was just how vulnerable she was to envy and disappointment, and that the high gloss of enthusiasm she'd brought to Hollywood had turned to dull fear. Expecting to meet others who shared her excitement, she'd been shocked by the indifference of those around her.

At eight forty-five, while the room filled, she'd offered a friendly hello to the well-dressed woman seated to her left. In response, Queenie had received a tolerant smile after which the woman turned rapt attention to the information sheet, circling certain speakers' names and their scheduled times to speak.

The conference had begun at nine. After the first ten-minute break, the woman had not returned to sit beside

Queenie. Queenie saw her up near the front talking earnestly to someone else. The new occupant of the seat beside Queenie came with a friend and paid Queenie no mind.

At the hour lunch break, most attendees had hurried purposefully from the conference room, while a small clot lingered near the speakers' platform. Mustering a weakening supply of courage, Queenie had applied a pleasant but serious veneer to her face and strode forward.

The group had peeled away from the platform the moment she arrived, and the illuminati had floated down each side of the untidy stage. She had stared straight ahead as if all along she'd chosen to arrive at this particular point to study emptiness. Maybe they would think her an avant-garde filmmaker pondering the use of an abstract, barren scene in her next film. Finally she had left, walking softly so as not to hear the hollowness of her footsteps.

Still, she'd returned hoping the afternoon would prove more fruitful, determined to make at least one friend.

The session began with an announcement that one of the featured speakers, a writer-director of household-word proportions, had canceled. Groans and a scooting of chairs followed, as a good dozen people left the conference. Queenie turned and smiled at the young man sitting beside her. That he might be an ax murderer entered her mind. Still, she asked what he thought of the conference. Visibly disgusted, whether with her or the change in program she didn't know, he shot from his chair and departed with a male companion.

At three o'clock, Queenie too had left . . .

She ordered a beer, then plopped down at an empty table where the umbrella shielded her from everything but the sun. Immediately, the bartender/waiter brought her iced beer and a frosted glass. She was glad he didn't pour while she searched in her satchel for money. It would have deprived her of something to do.

For a few moments she concentrated on her bottle and glass, as if transferring the beer from one to the other was inspired activity. She applied the same determination to taking the first sip, and felt great pleasure from the tart, cold beverage. Indeed, the beer had been costly. Next time, she'd be more careful with her money.

A chunk of tension slipped away, and for the first time she looked up and, to her surprise, directly into the eyes of a man sitting at a table opposite her own. She knew he'd been watching her since her entry into this otherwise solitary place, his court maybe. Something about him seemed familiar. Her eyes slid away toward the bar. By looking away, maybe she could see him better periferally, and discover the source of his familiarity. Then she realized it was his clothing: black trousers, a crisp white shirt, black vest, and red bow tie, an outfit identical to the bartender's.

Another mystery solved, she thought derisively.

"Waiting for Godot?"

Had he spoken to her?

"As long as you know he's not coming and realize that your purpose is simply to wait, you won't be disappointed."

His voice had the quality of a good massage; his accent was British. He seemed pleasant enough, but she hadn't spent several hundred dollars to meet a waiter or bartender. For considerably less, she could do just that down the street at Musso and Frank's. It hadn't occurred to her yet that it was unlikely an employee would be blatantly drinking on duty.

"Ready for another, Mr. Patterson?" the bartender asked, his quick eye noting the lonely ice in the man's glass.

"Fine, Jimmy. And if the woman so pleases, one for her as well." Mr. Patterson looked at Queenie, raising his eyebrows.

She stiffened defensively and glanced from one to the other of the identically clad men.

"Just come from there, haven't you?" Mr. Patterson nodded toward the conference room, his tone implying that it was some sort of battle zone.

She nodded.

"Well, bloody hell, have another drink!"

Then like some general concerned about his troops, he rose from the table and a moment later put a fresh bottle before her. Medal or weapon? she wondered.

Now that he was standing, who he was and why he'd been familiar finally impacted. A blush swept in a red rush from her chest to her scalp. In an effort not to appear totally dumbstruck and graceless, she stood and extended her hand. His was dry and firm. "You're Digby Patterson," she said. "Excuse me, I didn't recognize you at first."

"That was the intention—not that I'm constantly overwhelmed by drooling fans. But one never knows at these functions," he waved offhandedly toward the conference room. "And I prefer to choose my drinking companions."

"Would you like to sit down?"

"Thank you."

"Uh, you're speaking at four," she said nervously, knowing whatever she said would sound stupid.

He rubbed his temple, a gesture which, along with a mildly amused expression, she found disarming. "Yes, I suppose that's true. Honestly, though, I haven't a clue what to say." He frowned suddenly. "How long is it, incidentally?"

"How long is what?"

"My time."

"Oh!" Queenie pulled the folded sheet of pale green paper from her jacket pocket. "Uh, an hour. You're last."

He leaned forward to see for himself. "Dear God, you're right." Then he sat back, contemplating the tabletop, a frown deepening around a pair of hazel eyes. After a moment, his expression cleared and he smiled.

"To hell with it. You're . . ."

"I'm sorry. Queenie Davilov."

"Women named Queenie," he said deliberately, as if trying it on as a topic. "Let me think. . . . Queenie Leonard, one of the voices in *Alice in Wonderland*. A bird, as I recall. . . . Michael Korda's novel, *Queenie*. You, of course . . ."

"Don't forget the dogs," she added. "That's usually what people mention when I tell them my name."

He smiled. "And were you named after a dog?"

"A horse, Mr. Patterson."

"How delightful." He relaxed in his poolside chair. "You're luckier than I. My namesake was human and a twit, at that."

Queenie laughed.

"Except during the odd formal ceremony, I'm Digs."

"Odd formal ceremony," she thought. Two years ago he'd added an Oscar for Best Original Screenplay to various other honors.

"Any more at home like you?" he continued. "Maybe a Northern Dancer or a Secretariat?"

"A twin . . . Rajah—Raj for short. And a younger brother, Rex."

He raised his eyebrows. "Thoroughbreds?"

Queenie blushed. "Quarter horses." She paused then went on. "My mother, you see, believes the Davilovs were aristocrats who escaped the Russian revolution. I know you're a meticulous researcher, so before you ask, no. There's no proof."

"Why not do some checking? You never know, I may be talking to the next tsarina," he said with a twinkle.

"I'm afraid it's all a child's fantasy. Mother was shuttled out of New York on the Orphan Train. A farmer in Arkansas adopted her when she was only three. Whatever she invented was all she had."

"And your father?"

"That's easy. I'm a bastard."

"Well, there's something we have in common!" He raised his glass in a toast. "Just ask any of my ex-wives. Do you know your father?"

"No."

"Your mother ever have a horse named Stalin? He was a bastard, you know."

"He wouldn't count. Not to a monarchist like Mother."

Digby smiled. "She sounds an interesting character."

Queenie maneuvered the conversation back to his dilemma. "Why don't you talk about how you research your characters? I'm sure we'd all enjoy that."

"I appreciate your concern but I could never do that."

"Why not?"

"Good God, girl! Where's your sense of glamour? My job is to mystify the profession, present an arcane alchemical formula. The more incomprehensible the better. This is show business, after all. We must give them their money's worth."

They were silent for a moment. Digs studied her thoughtfully, then suddenly leaned forward. "Tell me, why did you pay good money to come to this conference?"

"Company, I suppose. I'm tired of feeling like the only

four-hundred-pound gorilla trying to push itself through a keyhole."

"You're joking?"

"Honestly, I thought I'd meet people like myself—just getting started. But everyone's so smug. No one's the least bit interested in, well, me."

"You're quite right. They want to meet someone like me, someone with connections who'll tuck them under an arm and make the going easy. Not only is it naïve, it's lazy. They've got more ego than brains. Look, Queenie, you're in a very long line, most of it clogged by morons waving trashy scripts, people who can't be bothered to learn the craft. What drives them is a crude desire to expose themselves in public and be paid handsomely for doing so."

Queenie sipped her beer. "Now that would be an interesting topic: screenwriters as exhibitionists."

"Christ," he snorted with a rueful laugh. "I was a reader at Fox for too long. It quite ruined any capacity I may have had for compassion. Tell me honestly, you didn't come here expecting to make a connection with some established producer, director, or lowly writer?"

"You're talking gravy. But realistically, the idea of meeting a few like-minded people, starting a production company and going our own way—"

"—is your idea of success?" he interrupted.

"My idea of success," she said more forcefully, "is being invited to speak at one of these conferences—and then declining."

He regarded her with astonishment, then suddenly laughed.

Queenie put several dollars on the table, then stood up. "Thank you for talking to me, Mr. Patterson."

"Wait," he objected. "Did I offend you?"

"Of course not. You've made me feel much better about being here. I just thought you might want to work on your speech."

"Oh, bloody hell. Do sit down. Wouldn't you like to know the secret of my success? I assure you, you won't hear it in the lecture hall."

"Of course I would." She resumed her seat.

"And do put your money away. Least I can do for your putting up with me is buy you a couple of beers."

"Let's leave it for a tip."

He sighed. "Suit yourself. Anyway, the first script I sold was the tenth I'd written. Instead of going to conferences and hoping to meet willing producers, I went someplace else. Can you guess?"

"I'd say you nailed your butt to a chair and didn't get up until you finished writing."

He brought out a frayed leather billfold fat with what might have been credit cards. Casually, he flipped them on the table; some were laminated, some were paper with worn edges. All were library cards.

"My passports to fame and fortune. Another person, celebrity or not, can only give you a piece of the world. The library gives you all of it."

Digby Patterson's image dissolved into the black night. Laughter drifted by. Queenie glanced toward the village, only a warm glow to her right. Someone was standing there, backlit by the glow. She started, giving a little gasp. Though she couldn't see the face, she felt certain the person had been staring at her. She blinked and the figure was gone. But she knew this was no trick of light, nor had she simply seen a tree and imagined a human figure. Trees don't have heads. And this head had been abnormally large and shaped like a light bulb.

She shook off a sense of foreboding and returned to her room. She had a script to read.

CHAPTER THIRTEEN

A SHARP SPEAR of morning light awakened Queenie. With a groan, she jerked up against the headboard, causing the few pages on her lap to slide to the floor. Another hundred-plus remained face-down, roughly stacked on the bed beside her. She slid off the bed, her feet sticking to two pages. She peeled them off and shuffled to the window to draw the curtain.

The villain in this scenario—an empty green wine bottle—stood on the nightstand. She picked it up with two fingers, as if it were infectious waste, and dropped it in the plastic-lined wicker basket. The filament in the bedside lamp still glowed, reminding her that she'd fallen asleep with the light on. She turned it off and glanced around the room, absently plucking her T-shirt from patches of damp skin.

Then the pain struck. It began just below her left eye,

carved a thirty-degree arc around the socket, then shot in random directions through her brain like white-hot light through a prism. She cursed her hand for raising the bottle too many times and her lips for welcoming the hand's offering. She stood quietly, waiting for the pain to withdraw, and rehashed the previous night's activities, remembering that before tackling the script, she'd made a thorough search of the room.

The parador had been booked for the exclusive use of the film company for several months. Patterson had lived in this room, on and off, during that time—that's what Freddie had said when he brought the script last night, along with the bottle of wine. But nothing remained, no toiletries in the bath, not a sheet of paper in the desk, not a forgotten sock beneath the bed. A couple of neatly folded blankets were in the wardrobe, but nothing else. She half wondered if he'd found a secret door therein and was now wandering around Narnia.

Queenie slogged to the bathroom and stripped while the sink filled with cold water. There was no shower, and a bath seemed more appropriate for a relaxing soak. She stuck out her tongue, recoiling slightly at the color. Even her teeth were tinted burgundy.

After mending and dressing the external flaws, she went downstairs for a light breakfast, which she hoped would cure the hangover.

Señora Pujol—who with her husband, the wiry little *portero*, ran the parador—orbited around Queenie like a binary star. Thanks to the señora's knowledge of English, seasoned with Spanish and Catalan, Queenie's informational landscape filled out: Freddie, the cast, and the crew had been shooting since dawn. She, Queenie, wasn't to be disturbed

9 9

until lunch. And most important, Queenie looked just like the señora's sister, Abril.

As the coffee penetrated the convolutions of Queenie's brain, and the tortilla settled her stomach, she began to feel more human.

"Señora, uh, do you remember Señor Patterson? The writer?" Queenie spoke slowly.

Señora Pujol nodded vigorously. "Sí, sí. I remember."

"Do you remember before he disappeared, uh, left? Did he act, well, different? You know sad, happy . . ." Queenie shrugged, decided against *preoccupied*.

"No. He same. Bery nice." Then she blurted, "You finish. Come with me?"

"Where?" Queenie asked, surprised.

"To see friend. *Por favor*."

Carrying several string bags, Señora Pujol bustled Queenie out of the parador. They hurried down the curving, dusty road and into the village where, at eight thirty, all the shops were open. A number of men sat outside the tavern drinking coffee and reading newspapers, their generous leathery noses poking out from beneath black berets worn low on their foreheads.

"I change his bed," Señora Pujol suddenly blurted.

"What?"

"Señor Patterson. I change bed."

"Okay." Queenie wondered what Señora Pujol was getting at. She took a few deep breaths of the crisp, pine-scented air to try and clear her head.

"Is, uh, strange. Bery strange." The señora frowned. "I do washing myself. Change beds. *Comprende?*"

"You do the laundry?"

"*Sí! Mira*, top sheet clean. No is . . ." She twisted the bottom of her calf-length black skirt.

"Crumpled? Wrinkled?"

The señora's face brightened. "*Sí!* Is . . ." She ran her hands across the skirt's rough woolen fabric.

"Smooth?"

"*Sí*. Smooth. Clean. Señor Patterson sheets *always*, uh, wrinkles. Messy, bery messy."

"When was this?"

"Uh, Saturday. Last."

"In the morning?"

She nodded impatiently, wanting to continue before she forgot the words. "*Mira*, one sheet is missing from all sheets."

They crossed the square, where an outdoor market bustled with activity and women shopped for fruit and vegetables and fresh fish from the coast. Queenie's head still felt misted by wine.

"I busy. Not think till now when you ask how he is being— sad, happy. *Mira*, he must sleep like this—" She suddenly stopped and went rigid, arms straight at her sides.

They walked behind the church, and passed the graveyard, where Señora Pujol crossed herself seemingly by rote.

"So, you're saying, you don't think he slept under the top sheet? Was the bottom sheet wrinkled?"

"Oh *sí*. Is wrinkled."

"And one sheet was missing from your inventory." What the hell was the woman talking about?

Señora Pujol tapped her head. "I count good. I know."

Another fifty yards and they came to a small house where smoke curled from the chimney. Queenie noticed some struggling tomato plants. She remembered her mother's juicy beefsteak tomatoes, and felt herself awakened by a pungent, remembered taste followed by an unexpected wave of homesickness.

She followed Señora Pujol, who entered by way of the kitchen. Crumbs from a fresh loaf of bread sprinkled the surface of a sturdy oak table stained by countless meals. A coffeepot whistled softly on a woodburning stove. The olfactory delights of coffee, fresh bread, and wood momentarily transported Queenie to the house in which she grew up.

"*Hola!*" Señora Pujol called out.

A tiny old woman with a face the color and texture of a peach pit emerged from an adjoining room. The two women spoke in rapid Catalan, and Señora Pujol motioned toward Queenie. The old woman looked Queenie over with skeptical black eyes. Finally, she shrugged then led them into a small bedroom.

A crucifix hung above a single bed where a young woman, maybe fifteen, lay under a rough woolen blanket. A narrow armoire stood on the other side of the room.

Señora Pujol spoke to the girl. This time Queenie caught a recognizable word—*doctor*. Instantly, she realized the mistake. Freddie must have told the señora that Queenie was the "script doctor," but only "doctor" had stuck in the woman's mind.

She noticed a Spanish-English dictionary and some back issues of *¡Hola!*, a popular Spanish magazine, on a small table along with a few cosmetics, among them a box of face powder. She moved toward the bed and beheld one of the healthiest teenage faces she'd ever seen—beneath the patina of powder. An idea popped into her head that might save the señora some embarrassment.

Queenie went through the motions of taking the girl's

pulse—strong—then put her hand upon the smooth fore-head—cool. She turned to Señora Pujol.

"Is there a doctor in the village?"

"*Sí*. He go many billage," she said making a circular motion with her hands. "Yesterday, he say Isobel is good. Uh," she nodded toward the tiny woman standing by the doorway, "I say American doctor at parador. Give second, uh . . ."

"Opinion?"

"*Sí!*"

"Well, ask, uh, Isobel, to have lunch with us today. I mean, if she feels up to it."

Señora Pujol frowned. Queenie said something about a little exercise and fresh air curing all sorts of teenage ills.

Señora Pujol translated but the girl's suddenly bright eyes suggested she already understood. Queenie offered to come back at noon, to be certain Isobel was strong enough for the outing.

On the way out, Queenie caught the eye of the old woman and thought she saw amusement but couldn't be sure. It could just as well have been outright suspicion.

Once they were out of the cottage and passing through the village, Queenie tried to explain "*script* doctor" to Señora Pujol. At one point Señora Pujol stopped and, grabbing Queenie's arm, stared up at her face as if trying to understand. Suddenly she let out a whoop of laughter. "Word doctor!" Then, her eyes clear with understanding, she squeezed Queenie's arm. "*Muy simpatico, guapa, muy simpatico!*"

They stopped at the outdoor market, Queenie tagging along as the older woman chose bunches of green onions with large white heads, several kilos of rich red tomatoes, garlic, and fresh anchovies. After the señora bought cheese and hard sausage at the butcher shop, Queenie helped carry the purchases back to the parador.

"Have you always lived here?" Queenie asked as they trudged up the dusty road.

"Oh no! Live many years in Barcelona. We take care of apartment building—where you stay."

"How did you get this job?"

"Don Carlos help us. We work for him many years."

When they reached the parador, Queenie requested a pot of fresh coffee, then went up to her room. She made the bed, and emptied the ashtray into the small wastebasket in which she'd deposited the wine bottle. She'd just begun to set up her work station on the desk when Señora Pujol arrived with a tray of coffee things. Queenie had to take a moment to reassure the señora she didn't want the bed changed, that she'd rather not be disturbed. Then she thought of something that might be important.

"Señora," she said as the woman began to leave, "what happened to Digby Patterson's clothes, papers, that sort of thing?"

The señora shook her head. "Nothing is here. *Nada.*"

"Not even toiletries—no razor, shaving cream?"

"*Nada.*"

"Did he bring much with him?"

"Clothes, no. Many papers, yes."

Queenie pointed to the fireplace. "What about ashes?"

Again the señora shook her head. "Is clean. All clean."

"Was his room key taken?"

"Keys all here. No key missing."

"Thank you, señora." Another thought struck her. "Was it warm last Friday night?"

The señora frowned.

"Maybe Mr. Patterson didn't need to use the top sheet because it was too warm."

She shook her head. "Night is cold." Then she added stubbornly, "And one sheet gone."

When Señora Pujol left, Queenie read the remaining script pages, and devoted the rest of the morning to a second, more concentrated study.

A little before noon she put aside her notes and, making certain she had money in her pocket, went down to the village.

She purchased a bottle of red wine at the bodega, then stopped at the outdoor market for half a dozen eggs and a kilo of fresh tomatoes. Flowers would have been nice but she had the feeling the old woman would prefer more utilitarian offerings. And too much would appear to be charity.

As she made her way to Isobel's, she was struck by the relative newness of all but a few cottages. She had expected all Spanish villages to be not just old but quite ancient.

A few minutes later, she arrived at the cottage. Deciding that an arrival at the kitchen might be an act of unwelcome familiarity, she presented herself at the front door. Isobel answered almost immediately. The white powder had been scrubbed off, leaving her skin a luminous rose color. Her black eyes were widely spaced and revealing of compassion and a certain playfulness. She wore her hair like Queenie's, in a single long braid.

Her grandmother, she said, had gone to the sanctuary.

Isobel took the food and wine into the kitchen while Queenie waited in a tiny living room. A few yellowed sheepskins were thrown over rough wooden chairs huddled around a cold black hearth built into the soot-streaked stone wall. An agonized Jesus hung from a nail. There were no books, magazines, nor television. An oil lamp, a box of kitchen matches, and a battered ashtray were set on a small table. It was then that Queenie realized the house had no electricity.

Isobel returned looking both shy and embarrassed. Queenie sensed something about to burst inside the girl.

"How are you feeling?" Queenie asked.

"Uh, is better."

At first, Isobel's English was punctuated by halts and hesitations. But once they were outside and had passed through the gate, Isobel changed, opening up like a time-lapse photographed flower.

Queenie learned that Isobel's father was a shepherd currently staying with his flock farther north, that her mother had died in a fall, and Isobel lived with her grandmother, who didn't like the film crew being there and even considered people in surrounding villages to be "foreigners."

Isobel attended a convent school in Gerona. The girls there made fun of her and others from remote villages, but lately had been unnaturally pleasant, giving her gifts of sweets. She knew why, of course. They wanted her to invite them to the village so maybe they could meet Tybalt St. Germain; some even thought she could get them a part in the movie. Since Isobel was unable to do anything of the sort, the girls had turned on her, accusing her of putting on airs. When she'd heard the cast and crew were returning, she'd feigned illness so she wouldn't have to endure the badgering of some, the insults of others.

"When I am very young I want to go to America. I study English. Señora Pujol, she help me. Sometimes I work at parador. Is very nice you to invite me lunch. Maybe is better I help Señora Pujol. I tell grandmother I work, not eat."

Queenie suddenly realized her mistake. A caste system

existed here. This being a small village, the grandmother would soon learn if Isobel ate with the "foreigners" rather than serving them. The girl would probably get into trouble for Queenie's generous though naïve invitation. Whatever Queenie might believe, it wasn't right to impose those beliefs in someone else's country.

"I apologize. Do what you think is right."

"*Gracias.*"

To one side of the parador, beneath an ancient and enormous oak tree, trestle tables were set up for an alfresco lunch. Señor Pujol, wearing his standard blue jacket and beret, worked at a couple of grills constructed from sliced oil drums.

Isobel served the table where Freddie, Nuria, Tybalt, Queenie, and Nathan were gathered.

The fare was simple and hearty, enhanced for Queenie by Isobel's commentary in English, while she named foods in Spanish and Catalan. Señor Pujol kept the *cebollas* coming, plates of grilled green onions that were eagerly and quickly consumed. There were large bowls of olives and baskets of *pa ab tomate*, bread slathered with ripe tomatoes. Queenie helped herself to anchovies marinated in olive oil and sliced garlic, and thinly sliced *jamón serrano* that had been sun- and snow-cured, its nutty flavor the result of pigs fed a diet of acorns.

Señora Pujol replenished the bottles of wine and pitchers of water to dilute the wine. Queenie stuck with water alone.

During the meal, Queenie caught snatches of Freddie and Nuria's conversation. Nuria expressed reluctance to shoot certain mountain scenes. Queenie wondered if those were the scenes she'd read, in which Cristiana had led those on death lists through the mountains at night. Having spent her childhood summers in the Pyrenees, Cristiana had known the paths well.

Again Queenie was puzzled by the apparent problems with the ending. By guiding people to the border and safely out of Spain, the woman clearly had shown a heroic character—especially given the fact that she herself had not sought that safety, but continuously returned to the village or to her nearby summer home. Hers didn't seem to be the actions of a fascist sympathizer.

At the end of the meal, while Isobel cleared off the table, Señora Pujol announced that coffee would be available on the front veranda, where those who wanted could relax and enjoy the siesta.

Gradually people began leaving the tables.

While daubing a piece of bread in olive oil, Queenie studied Isobel thoughtfully. "Isobel, do you ever go climbing?"

"Oh, yes," Isobel replied enthusiastically. "You want me take you?"

Tybalt immediately grasped Queenie's line of thought and turned to Freddie. "Freddie, we have a natural-born mountain goat here. Maybe she could double for Nuria."

Nuria suddenly perked, and regarded Isobel for the first time with interest.

"Her hair's too long," Freddie said.

Nuria left her seat and walked around to Isobel. In Spanish she told the girl to stand up. She and Nuria were about the same size and height.

"Christ, Freddie, put a wig on her," Tybalt said, finishing his meal.

"That would mean taking her to Barcelona," Freddie commented, no doubt thinking of the added expense—but he did seem interested in Isobel.

Considering the problems he'd already encountered, Queenie could understand his hesitation. At the same time, if anything happened to Nuria, if she fell and broke something, the film would be in big trouble.

"Then cut her hair," Tybalt said.

Queenie cringed at the thought of Isobel's magnificent mane being shorn for a few scenes in a movie. "What if she wore a scarf or a cap?" she suggested quickly. "Besides, it's more realistic. Cristiana guided those people at night and it was cold."

Freddie looked interested. "Yes . . . that would work."

So far, no one had asked Isobel, who stood wide-eyed and quivering with anticipation. Queenie considered the situation an example of the actor as "meat." And she was as much to blame as anyone, having thought of the girl in the first place.

"Don't get her hopes up," Queenie admonished Freddie. "If you want her, say so. Then ask if *she's* willing."

"You sound like a stage mum," Freddie retorted. Then he relented. "Nuria, ask the girl if—"

"She speaks English," Queenie said. "And her name's Isobel."

Freddie inclined his head. "Thank you, Ms. Davilov." Then he left his seat and spoke to Isobel.

And so, Isobel, who'd played hooky so as to avoid the cruel jibes of her classmates, now found that she was going to be in the movie herself. It was quite a turnaround for the girl.

Freddie instructed Nat to take care of the necessary release form, then took Queenie aside.

"Walk with me to the car." As they skirted a line of plane trees on the north side of the parador, he told her he was hand-carrying the negative of the film shot that morning to a lab in Barcelona. A local air courier service would be flying him to and from the city. Being on his guard, Freddie wouldn't entrust the job to anyone but himself.

"Shall I go with you?"

"No room. The plane's a two-seater." They passed the veranda, where a few people were relaxing during this, the siesta. "I should be back by six thirty. *Should.* If there's a problem, go on without me."

"Go on? Where?"

He shook his head slightly. "Sorry, I keep thinking you already know everything—we're dining with my brother tonight. He's just returned from Rome. Tell me, do you have something appropriate to wear?"

"I brought a cocktail dress."

"Marvelous," he said with obvious relief. "Carlos is every bit the old-fashioned don; believes in dressing for dinner and all that. Don't take me wrong, but be at your professional best. And I realize it's a little late to ask, but could you come up with some sort of ending? Anything within reason. We can make changes later. He wants proof that you can write."

"Why should he care?"

"Q," he said patiently—instinctively using the diminutive favored by those closest to her—"Carlos is the executive producer, given the title because, among other things, he organized the investment group that pays our bills."

Suddenly she realized just who this man was. "He defines arrogance," Michael deBeers had said. Of course! "*That* Carlos," she said. "The boy in the film!"

"Another thing. He's your Barcelona landlord. Owns the

two flats on the top floor. He's involved on many fronts. I daresay you can see now why he would care."

Freddie stopped at the edge of the graveled parking lot. In the distance, the bright blue waters of the Mediterranean drew the eye like a liquid magnet.

"Why don't we meet for a drink first, say sevenish? I'll go over what you've written before we leave."

"How much do you want?"

"Five to seven minutes should do."

Translated, a minute roughly equaled one typewritten, formatted page.

"No problem," she lied. But that's what script doctors were for: quick-and-dirty jobs. Whether you've got five days or five minutes, you'd better produce . . . and often by reading the director's mind.

"You wouldn't happen to have any books on the civil war?" she asked.

He frowned. "Just off the lobby you'll find a reading-cum-tea room. Might be some appropriate literature there."

"Well, I should at least see the location. How far is it?"

"As the crow flies, maybe a quarter of a mile. But the paths are overgrown and since we're not crows, the road's the easiest route; twenty minutes by car." He started to leave. "Nat will drive you—wouldn't want you getting lost."

CHAPTER FOURTEEN

WITH NAT IN command that's probably just what would happen—they'd get lost—Queenie thought a moment later while looking around the "reading-cum-tea room." Small end tables and floor lamps adjoined frayed but comfortable-looking chairs and settees. The low, beamed ceiling gave the room a snug, homey atmosphere. Ashtrays, magazines, and regional tour guides in various languages were scattered around the tables.

She stooped to inspect the three bookshelves built low to one side of the blue and white tiled fireplace. Stacked on top were board games—chess, checkers, and backgammon—and boxes of dominoes. The library mostly offered paper and hardback mysteries and thrillers, a few in English, French, and German, most in Spanish. Queenie noted the German translation of a mystery by Janet LaPierre, and several of Collin Wilcox's books, both American authors she liked.

Further on, she found *They Shall Not Pass*, Dolores Ibarruri's autobiography, which she'd used in college to research her short film on the woman. As she flipped through the book, an underlined passage caught her eye:

"Keep your powder dry and sleep with one eye open. The enemy lurks everywhere . . ."

The room darkened for a moment. A passing cloud? Queenie felt a slight chill and wondered who had thought the words important enough to highlight.

A few minutes later her search stopped with what appeared to be the only children's book here written in English, *Child of the Time*. She wondered if any children had gotten past the nightmarish cover, which featured a demonic-looking little boy with fangs and large ears. She shelved it and left the room with the only civil war offering she could find, in English anyway, the Dolores Ibarruri book.

A fat, beige rotary telephone sat on the reception counter in the small lobby. On her way upstairs to drop off the book, she stopped, considering making a call to Joey. As the West Coast editor for *World Abuzz*, Joey was tapped into the Hollywood gossip network and might have heard something about Digby Patterson. Joey kept erratic hours, but even so was not an early morning person. Figuring the time in L.A. to be between six and seven A.M., Queenie decided to wait, and hurried on upstairs.

Several minutes later, Queenie entered the kitchen hoping to get directions to the location from Señora Pujol or her husband; the señora being the likelier candidate as Queenie hadn't heard the señor speak a word of English—a word of anything, for that matter.

She found Nuria, Señora Pujol, and Isobel spouting Catalan at Isobel's grandmother. Queenie didn't need a dictionary to translate the situation. The scene itself told the story. Isobel was near tears. The old woman's expression was frozen. Apparently she wasn't going to allow Isobel to appear in the film despite much cajoling and waving of arms.

Isobel spied Queenie. A moment later, Queenie was dragged into the cacophonous conversation, with Isobel gripping her hand.

"She say I lie!" Isobel jerked her head in the old woman's direction. "Who wants stupid village girl in movie? She say I just no want go to school."

Nuria snapped at Queenie in rapid Catalan, then Señora Pujol.

"Hey, would everyone calm down?" Queenie admonished. Still the frightful yelling continued. She slapped her hands together. *"Muy tranquil!"* An all-purpose expression, it was like saying "Chill out," and seemed to work.

The room went quiet and the women all stared at Queenie.

Queenie took a breath. "Has Nathan brought the release form?" she asked Nuria.

"No."

"Well, why don't you find him and get it. That's some proof anyway."

Nuria left quickly. The old woman started to point a bony finger but Queenie grabbed the hand in both of hers and smiled. The old woman crackled something in Catalan, then sharply withdrew the feather-light assemblage of bones.

"She say you bad doctor," Señora Pujol interpreted. "And the movie is all lies. She no want Isobel part of lie."

"Tell her . . . tell her movies are like paintings—an artist's interpretation."

Isobel and Señora Pujol spoke to the old woman for a few

minutes. Nuria returned, slightly breathless, waving the piece of paper under the old woman's nose. The old woman batted it away. Queenie wondered if she could read.

Then she had an idea. "Did anyone tell her Isobel will be paid? Paid for spending a few hours climbing?"

The other women looked at each other. Señora Pujol explained. The old woman's eyes widened. She smiled, then put up a hand to shield her toothless mouth.

"And tell her, I personally will see that she gets a pair of false teeth."

The eyes got bigger as the bribe was related. Finally, the old woman relented. But first, she wanted to *see* some of this alleged money.

Nuria pulled a wallet from her shoulder bag and handed several one-thousand-peseta notes to the old woman.

Isobel smiled gratefully at Nuria. Queenie now asked Señora Pujol for directions to the location.

"I know!" Isobel said and grabbed her hand again. "I take you."

Now Nuria protested. Isobel needed to learn something about the character she would be playing. Isobel needed to be fitted. But Isobel had learned something about film in a very short time: having something others wanted, she could extract her price. They could wait for her. Indeed a minor lesson, but with major implications for a young woman who'd probably never felt power in her life.

And so the two set out.

Once the parador was out of sight, Queenie had the sensation of crossing into another dimension. Maybe some of Isobel's natural athletic ability and youthful enthusiasm rubbed off. Maybe spring's fecundity and the luminescent growth, each leaf and blade of grass vibrant with the aura of new life, invigorated her. Whatever, she felt the transformation deeply, in her very cells. She shed layers of "civilized" concerns and worries and lost her shadowy headache. Doubt dissolved and everything seemed possible.

Close on to the north, the Pyrenees rose like young gods, stalwart and constant, something to believe in when humans disappointed. Beneath her feet she could almost feel Gaia's steady heartbeat. Scarlet poppies and wildflowers were everywhere. To the east, the Mediterranean was a deep postcard blue. The air smelled delicious.

The sweet scent, Isobel said, came from the orange orchards south in Valencia. A southerly breeze blew the scent of the blossoms throughout Catalonia.

For the most part, the path was wide enough to accommodate a cart, though, as Freddie had said, it was mostly overgrown. At some points, Isobel took to narrow trails through stands of pine where they could hear small animals disturbed by their passing—according to Isobel, wild pigs and foxes.

Isobel glanced back several times.

"What is it?" Queenie finally asked.

Isobel put her fingers to her lips. Both women stood silently, listening. Queenie heard only the chattering and squawking of birds going about the serious business of their avian lives.

Isobel frowned. "Come," she whispered, and led Queenie off the path. They backtracked and hid in the trees. Queenie now heard someone hurrying down the path just a few yards away. Then she saw him dappled in the sunlight, his curls bouncing. Nat.

After he'd passed, Isobel motioned for Queenie to follow. Instead of returning to the path, she headed back the way they'd come, parallel to the path, brushing past sumac (which Queenie hoped wasn't poisonous), and weaving through stands of pine, passing surefooted among scattered rocks, and now descending. Queenie followed carefully, being more at home on the flat, concrete plains of Los Angeles.

In a few minutes, they stopped outside the mouth of a cave concealed by a pile of rocks and a giant oak tree, the girth of which was three times as wide as the cave mouth.

"Isobel. I wanted to go to the village. The location."

"Sí. I know other way. Secret way." She smiled mischievously then darted into the dark mouth.

"I don't have a light."

"Is okay. I see."

By the faint outside light, they made their way to a tunnel of smooth hard-packed earth, obviously man-made. Queenie realized it must have been in use for centuries.

"Does this tunnel come from the parador?" she asked the darkness.

"Sí. Goes to old village." Queenie could barely see, but slowly became accustomed to shuffling behind Isobel's presence more than her form.

"When I am young, I play in here. Steal oranges from kitchen in the parador. I think Señora Pujol, she know. But she say nothing. Señora Pujol *muy simpática.*"

Queenie felt that Isobel kept talking more to use her voice to guide than to inform.

In a short time, they climbed worn stone steps, emerging behind the altar in a tiny crumbling church. Picking their way through heaps of rubble, they came to a gaping hole in the wall and jumped down into a graveyard.

For a moment, an unwelcome and surprising sense of gloom overwhelmed Queenie.

Isobel studied her face, then regarded the village itself, visible on the other side of the graveyard—the facades of whitewashed buildings huddled around an empty square, narrow streets winding up the south face of a craggy mountain. It seemed abnormally quiet, devoid even of the chatter of birds.

Isobel said softly, "Is strange." Then she made a motion toward her heart. "Feels bad, no?"

CHAPTER FIFTEEN

THERE IS SOMETHING subtly disturbing about a ghost town. Even movie sets do not, when empty, provoke the same feeling. The latter are meant to be hollow; all facade, empty of substance. But a place once lived-in retains some essence of former inhabitants. The haunting question when one sees something abandoned is, *why?*

Looking straight ahead, Queenie could see where the road entered from the southeast. About halfway down, two men were busy reloading the equipment truck after the day's shoot.

Unlike Señora Pujol at the graveyard near the Parador, Isobel did not cross herself when they passed the ancient plot where weeds and wildflowers grew between shattered grave markers and the occasional leaning rough-stone cross. Freddie had not shot the burial scene here, no doubt because he was unwilling to disturb the truly buried.

"Are you a Catholic?" Queenie asked.

"*Sí*." She glanced up at Queenie and smiled. "But no good Catholic. Many people, many, umm, beliefs." She shrugged. "All belief good. So, I am bad Catholic!"

Queenie laughed, which seemed to delight Isobel. The girl pointed at Queenie's heart, then her head. "You? Catholic? Belief?"

Uh-oh, Queenie thought. This could get me run out of Dodge. As they passed the crumbling ruin of the church, she noted the buttressed scaffolding that supported the facade on the other side. She briefly imagined hooded inquisitors carrying blazing torches and chasing her through the dark mountains.

"What I believe is older than the Catholic Church." She hesitated, unsure how to explain. She rarely talked about her beliefs, but then few people ever asked. "My beliefs are—" She searched for the equivalent Spanish word.

Isobel regarded her intently, apparently interested in the answer.

"*Feminista*," Queenie said, then repeated the word. "Yes. *Feminista*. But I don't think you should tell your grand-mother."

Isobel laughed. "Grandmother believe in spirits . . . and Samjaza. She acts good Catholic but she go to sanctuary. You go to Montserrat?"

Queenie shook her head. "Not yet."

"Black Madonna there. Is beautiful."

Leaving the graveyard, they paused and regarded the ghost town/movie set. Spanish names of businesses had been sten-ciled on windows, along with plastic displays that would be sprayed or rubbed with oil when the cameras rolled. The set director had done an excellent job of giving each building a lived-in look: mossy rooftops, stained and weathered facades, steps reconstructed to appear smoothed by time and activity.

"What happened to the people who lived here?"

"Grandmother say they bad . . . Samjaza take them. You know?"

"Samjaza?" Queenie shook her head.

"*Diablo.*"

"The devil?"

"*Sí.* Yes. Grandmother say the devil take them. They bad people."

"They did have a church," Queenie said, nodding back at the structure.

"Most village have church."

"What do you think?"

Isobel's eyes widened; apparently she was surprised to have been asked for her opinion. "Is not religion, is politics. In civil war, Grandmother say, people here, this village blow up convent—parador—where you stay they kill all nuns. When fascist come, fascist kill all people here because kill nuns. Understand?"

"Retaliation, reprisals. Is it true? I mean, is there proof that the people here murdered the nuns?"

Isobel shrugged. "Grandmother say. People here anarchists."

Queenie had read enough to know that churches were sacked, priests and nuns massacred because the church had sided with the monarchists and fascists. She momentarily envisioned the parador filled with screams and awash with blood. And if ghosts existed, there must be plenty haunting the rooms and corridors of the restored building. Gaia, *Earth*, had memory. And how blood-soaked that memory must be.

Within a few minutes they came to the end of the town,

where a meadow sloped into a valley. Queenie noticed a scorched patch farther down and figured it marked the place where the truck carrying all the equipment had burned. A costly disaster. Since technical equipment is usually rented, in essence, Freddie's insurance carrier had bought everything that had been destroyed. That one act could have stopped production. Accident or sabotage? Queenie wondered.

Nearby, an oak hovered over the small white crosses that marked the faux graveyard where Freddie had shot Cristiana's burial scene.

Queenie turned to Isobel. "Your village seems quite new compared to this place."

"Sí. Before civil war is only few shepherds. Is where grandmother live. This village," she pointed down the earthen street, "have market and school. Pero, after all people die, my village grow."

"Why wasn't this village rebuilt?"

"Very bad place. No one come."

The two entered the little graveyard. Queenie examined the small crosses but, oddly, could not find Cristiana's. She tried to recall its position as she'd seen it in the video. Her search was interrupted by the sound of someone's approach. Queenie and Isobel turned around.

"How'd you get here so fast?" Nat asked, his face flushed. Isobel eyed him with obvious distrust.

"A good guide," Queenie said evenly.

"Just wanted to make sure you didn't get lost. I, uh, heard what Nando said before he took off for the airstrip."

"We go back now?" Isobel asked. "For fitting?"

"You're right, we should get back," Queenie said, thinking of the work that lay ahead.

Isobel headed straight for the old mule track, apparently

unwilling to share the shortcut with Nathan, who, uninvited, joined them. But more than likely, Nathan knew about the old tunnel, especially if he'd been around while the set was being constructed.

"Looks like you're getting your exercise today," Queenie remarked as they trudged up the old more-or-less overgrown track.

Nathan didn't reply, though he did try to engage Isobel in conversation. Queenie was amused by Isobel's outright rejection of Nathan's attempts at flirtation and contented herself with devising scenes for Carlos Ballester's benefit.

Queenie wondered if Patterson had talked to Isobel's grandmother in the course of his research, but she refrained from asking with Nathan present.

She received the summons at quarter of seven while adding the last hairpins to the braided bun twisted at the back of her neck. Nathan, acting as gofer, looked somewhat startled to see her above eye level, as her three-inch heels elevated her height to six-one. Add to that the long-sleeved black Rosemarie Reed cocktail dress, the hair sleeked back, and a pair of baroque pearl earrings Dick had brought her from Japan the previous year, and she appeared quite formidable.

"I'll be right down," she said and closed the door in Nathan's face.

Freddie sat at the far end of the otherwise vacant veranda scribbling in a notebook, a glass of wine on the adjacent table. A cart with wine, a coffee urn, cups, and glasses was set nearby.

He placed the notebook on the table and stood up as she approached with the freshly typewritten sheets in hand. For a moment he regarded her with open admiration. "You look very smart, Q," he said, a thanks distinct in his voice. She wondered if he'd expected her to wear some bizarre California concoction.

"What can I get you? Wine, a coffee? A word to the wise: Señora Pujol's coffee's abominable. During the civil war they made it out of acorns. Frankly, I think they still do around here."

"Wine, then. Thank you," she said though the coffee she'd drunk that morning hadn't been all that bad. Of course it was much weaker than the syrupy concoction obviously preferred by Freddie.

"Red or white?"

"*Sangre de Toro*," she said, feeling a bit full of herself. But she was taken aback when he brought a bottle with just that on the label. A dry, full-bodied red from Miguel Torres.

"Wow. I thought I was just being cute."

"The vintner is Catalan. From Penedés, south of Barcelona. Cheers."

They clinked glasses.

"What did you think of the location?"

"If that was rubble when you bought it, then your set designer's a genius."

That brought a rare, bright smile. The first, in fact, she'd seen lighten the hollows on a face she suddenly realized was quite handsome.

"One question, though. I can understand refraining from shooting the burial scene in the actual graveyard—out of respect for the dead as well as for reasons of authenticity—but I'm curious. Where was Cristiana buried?"

The smile quickly vanished. "No one seems to know. But

bodies of traitors were often dumped in shallow graves, that sort of thing." He cleared his throat, then continued. "However, wolves were likely to dig up and eat the remains of those not allowed the requisite six feet under."

They were silent for a moment. Finally, Freddie said, "Frankly, I didn't want to be *that* authentic. I found a nice patch, gave her a view."

"I couldn't find her grave marker."

"What?"

"When I visited the location. I couldn't find a cross with her name on it."

"That's odd. Maybe someone pinched it—for a sort of souvenir." He looked into his wine and swirled it absently. "Rather a queer place, isn't it?"

"Peaceful—in an uneasy way."

"Every living inhabitant—man, woman, and child—was either shot or hacked to bits. Place was never scavenged—at least by humans—the rubble was left the same as it had been that fateful day. Well, at least until I came along."

"When did it happen?"

"February nineteen thirty-nine."

Queenie related what Isobel had said during their trek through the old village about it being a "bad place."

"These people live close to the land. Despite the church, I imagine a good number are pantheists. Old ways die hard in the country. Religious changes occur in cities, as often as not for political reasons." He took a deep breath. "Well now, what have you got for me?"

Queenie handed him the seven typewritten sheets, having surprised herself by the output. He read to the tune of crickets chirruping in the still, breathless early evening. She sipped her wine, also drinking in the view of the Costa Brava. From this distance, it appeared to be an artful animation set with tiny patches of white bordering a blue-green glass sea.

Freddie folded the pages lengthwise and put them inside his dinner jacket. He picked up his wineglass and stood up, motioning her to join him. They walked out on the soft, green grass to a bougainvillea sporting new purple blooms. He casually looked around as if admiring the view.

"Anything interesting in Digs's room?"

"*Nada*. By the way, have you notified the local authorities, talked to his family or anyone?"

"Last night, as a matter of fact, I had a discreet word with the local gendarmes. They're checking to see if he's left the country. His family, well, consists of a pack of ex-wives, all actresses. We must be circumspect, you know. Don't want the press suddenly descending on us." Queenie felt a twinge of relief that she'd decided not to call Joey. At the same time, Joey was an excellent source, and after all, detective work required making inquiries. Sooner or later, she'd have to shake the bushes.

They were silent a moment. Queenie was suddenly anxious to hear his thoughts on the scenes she'd written. She shifted her weight from one foot to the other, reminded of why she rarely chose to wear confining shoes.

Finally, she had to ask, though indirectly. "If your brother doesn't like what I've written, will I be off the project?"

Freddie didn't answer.

"Look, we both know Andrew Coachman wants the job back. What if he talks to your brother—"

Freddie raised a hand. "Let's wait until you've met Carlos. No sense worrying about the milk *before* it's spilled."

Nat appeared, dressed in a seersucker jacket, a blue-and-red Hawaiian shirt, beltless baggy pants bunched at the ankles of untied black-and-white soccer shoes. The clothes were artfully wrinkled, appearing to have been recently discovered under a rock pile. He said Nuria and Tybalt were ready. Freddie handed him the car keys.

"Might as well bring the car round."

Queenie and Freddie watched Nat's departure as they moved back to the veranda.

"My God," Freddie remarked. "The young today dress with their eyes closed."

She understood now why he might have expected her to dress less than conservatively. "Well, it certainly amazes me that a jerk like him has no worries about job security," she said, still miffed.

"Nepotism keeps him employed," Freddie retorted irritably. "Movies are about sacrifice. If I have to put him on the payroll to get this film made, then he's on!"

They left their glasses on the table. Freddie picked up the notebook.

"Freddie?"

He turned to look at her, his eyes hard.

"You haven't said a word about the scenes I wrote."

He looked surprised, his expression softening slightly. "Oh. Yes, well, they'll do nicely for our purposes."

This was not a man to quell anxiety by the use of a compliment. Even flattery would be okay, she thought grimly. Oh well, Davilov, you'll find out soon enough.

CHAPTER SIXTEEN

QUEENIE SMILED AT the very short woman bussing Freddie's cheeks. Probably in her early thirties, she was a deeply tanned, stylishly coiffed blonde wearing a backless amber dress. A five-carat diamond overloaded her ring finger and could have doubled as a searchlight.

"Muncie, this is our new writer, Queenie Davilov. Queenie, my sister-in-law, Montserrat Ballester."

"It's a pleasure to meet you Señora Ballester," Queenie said. She could see a faint resemblance to Nathan in the small black eyes and weak chin.

"Please. Call me Muncie," her hostess replied, offering neither her hand nor her cheeks. She turned to Freddie. "Carlos is in the study."

"I'll just show Queenie round the house, if I may."

But their hostess had moved enthusiastically to greet the others, Tybalt in particular. A servant appeared with glasses of sherry on a silver tray. Drink in hand, Freddie guided Queenie through the various large, airy rooms of the ground floor.

"This was my mother's summer place. Built at the turn of the century. We shot most of the love scenes here."

Far from the ostentation of Montserrat Ballester's diamond, the house reflected simpler tastes: polished hardwood floors, scattered wool rugs, sturdy furniture, shuttered windows, and bright watercolors of the region.

They stopped at a fireplace inlaid with decorative tiles. Above it hung a large painting of a fishing village at sunset, the buildings and surface of the sea a burnished red. Freddie lit his Dunhill and Queenie's pre-rolled variety, of which she had a small supply squirreled in her dress pocket.

"Your brother didn't mind?"

"Mind?"

"Shooting the love scenes here. After all, we're talking about his mother and her lover—not his father."

Freddie smiled slightly. "Over fifty-five years have passed. And anyway, he spends little time here. He has another house outside Barcelona, a flat in the city, and one in Rome."

"Was he here or in Barcelona when your mother died?"

"Here. Cristiana, Hannah, Jordi—his tutor—all stayed here through the winter of 'thirty-seven, 'thirty-eight. Ian visited on and off."

A thought struck her, causing a slight shiver. "Freddie, were you born in this house?"

He seemed surprised. "Why, yes. I was." He shook his head slightly. "Funny, I never think about that. Carlos told me Hannah and a woman from the village delivered me." Unexpected emotion seemed to overcome him. He passed through French doors out onto the veranda.

After a moment, Queenie joined him. "Can I get you another sherry?" she asked, as a means of finding out if she'd inadvertently touched a raw nerve—if he wanted to be alone.

"What?" he said, startled. Then he lightly touched her arm. "Sorry. A momentary lapse. Uh, they waited, you see, until I was born to arrest her."

The air smelled of the jasmine that entwined the pillars set at three-meter intervals along the length of the wide veranda. In the distance, the lights of the coastal playgrounds were coming on.

"After dinner we'll all troop back to the parador to screen the rough cut I brought back from Barcelona. I suppose then we'll see if Carlos minds."

"When were you born?"

"January third, nineteen thirty-eight."

"And she died . . ."

"February—"

"Ah, Fernando."

Both Queenie and Freddie turned. Queenie had the feeling the man had been standing behind them for several minutes before announcing himself. He stepped out onto the veranda and joined them. He and Freddie shook hands.

"Carlos," Freddie said, his voice cracking. He cleared his throat and introduced Queenie. "Our new writer."

"I've been looking forward to meeting you," Carlos said coolly.

"Freddie's just been showing me around. You have a lovely place here."

He shrugged. "This is nothing." By his flat tone, she could tell the statement didn't convey modesty. He meant it.

"How was Rome?" Freddie asked.

While the two men perfunctorily discussed Carlos's recent business at the Vatican, Queenie studied their host.

Carlos Ballester had thin lips, which always made her think of politicians—and anyone else who lied for a living. At one time a war had been waged on his face, in the pits on his cheeks and the trenches around his mouth and across his high forehead; maybe pubescent acne, maybe smallpox. He was tall, tanned, and fit. Though she knew he was in his late sixties, he had the body of a much younger man. Wearing an elegant gray silk suit, white shirt, and black tie with an understated silver pinstripe, he overpowered his surroundings, the *nobleza castral*, an old term meaning the "lord of his castle."

After a few moments, the servant announced dinner. Queenie saw Freddie pass Carlos the typewritten sheets, which were discreetly tucked away in the older man's jacket.

At dinner, Queenie found herself picking at her food. She should have been hungry but maybe the pompous atmosphere spoiled her appetite. Unaccustomed to the trappings of elegant dining—the heavy silverware, the china, the cut-crystal wine and water goblets, the rich and sumptuous meal—she found herself in a somber mood comparing rich and poor, sated and starving. It didn't help that she was seated beside Nathan on the right and a man on her left who ignored her completely.

Directly across the table, Nuria ate with the same lack of enthusiasm. At one end of the table, Señora Ballester—Muncie—chatted with Tybalt on her right, and occasionally smiled at Nathan on her left. At the opposite end, Carlos talked with Freddie and two other elegantly dressed men Queenie had never seen before, and whom she guessed were a couple of the film's investors.

Postprandial brandies and coffees were served in the living room with the tiled fireplace. Nuria took her snifter and wandered outside.

Queenie approached Freddie. "Look, I'd like to talk to your brother but I've got the feeling I'm supposed to make an appointment."

"I'll see what I can do." Queenie watched Freddie and Carlos. Neither man looked at her. A moment later, Carlos left. Freddie mingled briefly then joined Queenie.

"Come with me."

The two of them went up the stairs off the foyer. They passed several bedrooms, then entered a study at the end of the hall. French doors led to a balcony that ran the length of the room. A fire crackled in the hearth. A floor lamp added extra light. The walls were covered with framed photographs of Carlos with such dignitaries as Pope John Paul II, Felipe Gonzales—Spain's Socialist prime minister—England's former Prime Minister Margaret Thatcher, and an assortment of other business and political leaders. Most curious though, was a case filled with a much different assortment, figures of a curiously scatological preoccupation.

"Some people collect Lladros," Freddie said, referring to the world-famous figurines. Those on display, though, were far from the graceful beauty of ballerinas and shepherdesses. "These are called *caganers*, uh, 'shitters.' "

A pile of excrement was connected to the bare buttocks of each squatting individual. Beneath a floppy red stocking cap

Freddie called a *barrentina*, each figure wore an expression of concentration, some bordering on ecstasy.

"They're reflective of the Catalan philosophy of man's connection to the earth. In shit, man is returning to the earth the nourishment the earth gave him. It's a theme you'll find in the works of Dalí and Joan Miró, both men, of course, Catalan."

"What about Gaudí? Could he have intended the Sagrada Familia to be some sort of monumental pile of shit?"

Carlos laughed. Queenie started, unaware of his presence. He entered the room from the balcony. Again she wondered how long he'd been watching and listening.

"Quite a few people believe it to be just that," he commented. "Do you find them offensive?"

"Not at all." She thought of the high-dollar gourmet food stores in L.A. that sold jewelry made of cow dung.

Then Carlos took Queenie by the arm and guided her out onto the balcony. She heard the door close and realized Freddie had left.

"Are you enjoying Spain?"

"So far, the job has precluded, uh, pleasure. But then, I wouldn't trade places with any other writer."

"Apparently, your predecessor didn't share your feelings."

"Digby Patterson or Andrew Coachman?"

His thin lips lengthened in what she assumed to be a smile of micromillimeter width. "Señor Coachman was a mistake—an expensive one. Why on earth did Fernando hire another writer when he himself was not even here to confer with him? Coachman simply began rewriting the original script—scenes that had already been filmed! Such a waste!"

Queenie wondered how Carlos knew what Andrew had been writing. Hadn't she heard he'd been in Rome?

"No, I was referring to Señor Patterson," Carlos went on.

"You must have spent a lot of time together while he was researching the script."

"As much as possible. I'm a very busy man."

"I'd like to hear your account of what happened to Cristiana." They stood at the wrought-iron railing, overlooking a garden that seemed to extend all the way to the Mediterranean. Queenie saw Nuria, who was standing by some garden chairs, suddenly glance up at them, then scurry back into the house. Oddly, Nuria had been scowling.

Carlos sniffed the bouquet captured in his balloon glass, then carefully sipped the brandy. She was beginning to think he hadn't heard her, or maybe chose not to answer.

"I know it must be painful—"

"Time releases pain," he retorted, sounding almost resentful. "You imply that outside forces were charged with her fate. That's not true. She was responsible for her own— and the deaths of others. The gun might well have been in her own hand."

"Were you there . . . the day she died?"

"Yes, though I did not witness the execution. I heard the shots. Three. Hannah and I came at dawn to say good-bye. I remember it was a cold day. It had snowed the night before. Shortly after, we returned to the summer house."

"When, I mean, what date?"

"February fifth, nineteen thirty-eight."

The date tweaked something in her memory. She wondered why it would be familiar. Maybe something she'd read in the past while making the Dolores Ibarruri film. She made a mental note to check into it.

"Tell me, if she hadn't been shot what do you think would have happened to her?"

"She would have been imprisoned or executed. Many were, and many went into exile, unable to return until Franco's death in nineteen seventy-five." He paused, then said with something akin to admiration, "Franco was a very powerful man. Did you know that in the mid-fifties, I believe it was nineteen fifty-four, Pope Pius XII declared him to be the Primate of All Spain."

"Sort of like the great ape?"

He jerked his head toward her angrily. "*Chica*, you are disrespectful—like so many Americans. What do you know?"

"You're right. Americans hold dictators in low regard." Then she thought it best to return to the subject of Cristiana. "Your mother, did she like Franco?"

"My mother would have liked anyone who kept her in food, wine, and beautiful frocks."

"But if she sympathized with Franco, then why do you think she would have been imprisoned—or executed? And if her only interests were pleasure, why did she endanger herself by guiding people over the Pyrenees?"

He answered with an impressive shrug. Either he hadn't known his mother very well, or he was hiding something.

"Do you have photographs, diaries?"

"My father destroyed all photographs. As for diaries, she wasn't inclined that way."

"Surely, the newspapers had pictures of her—your parents being important members of society and all."

"*All* photographs were destroyed," he said pointedly. His father must have been powerful indeed to arrange for newspapers to destroy their photos. And maybe he'd had help from Franco's Nationalists.

"Were you close to her?"

"What adolescent is close to his parents? As a small boy,

I suppose. She enchanted all she met. A woman with more spirit than moral character. She had what we Spanish call *duende*, roughly a sort of charisma."

"Have you seen the dailies?"

"Not all but some."

"Are you happy with the casting—Nuria in particular?"

"Of course. I chose her myself."

"Hmm. I'm curious why you'd cast an unknown in such a meaty role. Why not someone like, say, Victoria Abril?"

"Ah, you are familiar with Spanish actresses."

"I saw *Tie Me Up, Tie Me Down*," she replied quickly. "You still haven't answered my question."

He stiffened and she wondered if she'd gone too far. In essence, Carlos Ballester was her boss.

"What do you think about all these, uh, accidents?"

"Incompetence," he replied abruptly. "Costly incompetence. Fortunately, the film is completed—but for Fernando's inability to finish."

"Are you anticipating a Palme d'Or?" she asked, deciding it best to ignore what he'd said about his brother. *Half*-brother.

He glanced at her abruptly. By the look on his face, he didn't seem to know what she was talking about.

"The highest award at the Cannes Film Festival."

"Of course," he said with a snort. "Budget concerns have preoccupied me." He finished his brandy. "Now I must get back to the other guests."

"One more question, Señor Ballester."

He regarded her coldly; not a man used to being detained once he made up his mind to leave.

"What ending do you envision? The, uh, resolution."

"My mother's death ends the film!" Even in the dim light,

she could see color infusing the pockmarked face. "It should be left at that. All this bother about a betrayal is nonsense and, more important, a waste of money. Fernando wanted to make a film. Well, he's made the film. He says he still needs a scriptwriter but I don't think so."

Queenie started. "Meaning?" She found herself trembling.

"The meaning is clear, *chica*." He shifted smoothly into the role of diplomat. "We are, after all, talking business. You are welcome to stay and enjoy my study."

Then he left her.

Had the crack about the "great ape" doomed her? She wasn't sorry she'd said it. More than that, she wondered why Ballester, as a staunch Catalan, would take offense. The thought occurred to her that, if Ballester was the only source of information, Digby Patterson must have had a hell of a time filling out the character of Cristiana. But being an adherent to the philosophy of machismo, Señor Ballester might have been more forthcoming with another male.

After a moment, she went to find Freddie, having had enough of framed dignitaries and little shitting men.

CHAPTER SEVENTEEN

SHE FOUND FREDDIE on the veranda, he and Muncie wrapped in the fabric of the jasmine's heavy scent.

"Excuse me, may I speak to you a moment, Freddie?"

Acting the perfect hostess, Muncie excused herself and went inside.

"I'm not exactly sure, but I think your brother may have fired me."

"Oh bloody hell! What for?"

"According to him, the film's wrapped, and the services of a scriptwriter are no longer needed."

"I'd better talk to him."

Not feeling inclined to socialize, Queenie moved to the grouping of outdoor furniture and sat down. Her feet hurt. She kicked off her shoes and gripped the cool grass with her toes. While Carlos might be a great businessman, it took a producer with experience to understand the machinations of the movie business. Of course, maybe he had run out of cash and this was his way of admitting it. And too, this might be some power struggle between Freddie and Carlos, with Carlos flexing his muscles when things weren't going smoothly. Unfortunately, ego battles forced everyone to lose sight of the purpose—to make a movie.

"Ah, the heir presumptive."

"Excuse me?" Queenie replied, not welcoming the interruption, even if the interrupter was Tybalt St. Germain standing a little unsteadily. She'd noticed him guzzling his wine at dinner.

"Fed up with the lot of us, already?"

"Just thinking."

"May I join you—not that I'm at all interested in thinking."

"Go ahead."

He moved a chair closer to hers.

"You look quite stunning tonight."

"Thank you."

"And if I say so, the only sane addition to our little dysfunctional film family."

"Why do you say it's dysfunctional?"

"Well it is that! And so bloody incestuous what with Nuria screwing our rather insufferable executive producer, *his* wife casually feeling me up during dinner—and planning some sordid rendezvous after the old sod goes to bed. The thought of getting sloshed as a way out is rather revolting. But there it is. Kindly write me out of this scene . . . please?"

"You're an actor, Tybalt. Do your stuff."

He caught her eye. "You don't know Muncie. A wicked, wicked woman if she doesn't get her way. Now *there's* an actress."

Now she understood why Nuria had been so remote during the evening. "Does she know about Nuria and Carlos?"

"Of course. Silly of Nuria to act so aloof. Muncie finds it most amusing."

"But doesn't care?"

"Absolutely not. She's in for the money, luv, could care less where his dick finds shelter. And Carlos is too full of himself to believe his wife would be remotely interested in any other male." Then he concluded forlornly, "Even me."

"The other man," she said and gave him an amused smile.

"For once, trying not to be."

Freddie hurried toward them. "Time to break up this party," he announced. To Tybalt he said, "Muncie's looking for you . . . something about you driving her car."

"I'm riding with you!" Tybalt declared, lurching to his feet. "I'm in no fit state to be driving."

Queenie rose and Freddie took her by the arm, practically running around the side of the house while Tybalt followed. She wondered how much was acting and how much was really wine.

"Am I still employed?"

"Only just. I'll explain in the car. Christ, I hate producers who interfere. Just do me a favor, Queenie."

Back to "Queenie," is it? she mused. "Sure."

"Stay the hell out of his way."

Tybalt lounged in the back seat of the Jaguar while Queenie sat beside Freddie. They'd left the others to sort out who rode with whom to the parador. Freddie didn't speak until they were well on the winding road that would take them the five plus miles to the parador.

". . . told him I absolutely had to have you on the set for rewrites, that half your fee had already been paid, that if you left now, he would have given away his money—no doubt my most convincing argument."

"What did our Carlos do—give Queenie the sack?" Tybalt piped up.

Ignoring Tybalt, Freddie asked a question of his own. "What was it you said that made him so furious?"

Tybalt moved up between them and patted Queenie on the shoulder. "Not to worry, luv. Sacked me twice, didn't he, Freddie? I think our Nuria is the only one to escape his wrath. But we know the reason for that, don't we?"

"Oh, do be quiet, Tybalt," Freddie snapped, then glanced at Queenie. "Well?"

Queenie shrugged. "I was only trying to get some information about Cristiana. I did make a remark about Franco." She briefly related the conversation and her interpretation of the Primate of All Spain.

Tybalt let out a hoot.

"Christ," Freddie hissed, obviously not sharing Tybalt's amusement.

"Well, he's Catalan! I figured they all thought Franco was less than human. Look how he suppressed the culture and language."

"Queenie, Franco did rule this country," Freddie said evenly. "Look, I may not like the royal family but I don't take it too well when an outsider makes a rude comment about the queen."

"Oh all right. It wasn't very tactful. Just seems odd that he'd be defensive about, of all people, Franco. If it wasn't for Franco his mother—and yours—might have had a much longer life."

A silence fell. Queenie stared ahead watching the car's headlights burn a narrow trail into the darkness that fell around them. Tybalt whistled tunelessly.

"Look," Freddie finally said, "without Carlos this film would never have been made—at least not here. He arranged for the Spanish crew, the parador, took care of the endless bureaucratic nonsense required for outsiders to work here—not to mention putting together an investment group. One word from him and we're all on the next plane out of Spain."

Around eleven, the group finally settled in for the screening set up in the reading-cum-tea room. While they'd been at dinner, the Pujols had rearranged the furniture and brought in the drinks cart. Queenie was pleased to find a fresh pot of coffee, though mostly the others chose not to interrupt the intake of alcohol.

While waiting for Carlos and the others to arrive—Freddie confirmed that the two other men were indeed investors—Queenie managed to corner Señora Pujol for a moment, to inquire about making telephone calls. An idea had begun to take root, and she thought a call to Michael deBeers might be of help.

The señora produced a notebook in which everyone logged and initialed the calls they made. For budget purposes, once the film wrapped each person would be charged for personal calls, though the production company would absorb those made for business purposes. It was based on the honor system. Still, if there was any suspicion that someone had been making personal calls and charging them to business, accounting would find out eventually, and that individual would also incur a steep fine for abusing the trust.

The rest of the party arrived. The call to Michael would have to wait. But there was no urgency. Just an idea.

Once everyone had taken a seat, Nat doused the lights. Expectantly, the group watched the numbers tick off on the leader, then . . .

The film opened with a tracking shot through heavy mist, the background formless shadow; the sound of someone panting and running through heavy brush. Then, in a voice over, Hannah called out, *"Cristiana! Cristiana!"*

Music, titles, and credits would be added during post-production work.

The scene cut to a close-up of a young girl wearing a black blindfold and counting backward. "Ten, nine, eight . . ."

Again the misty tracking shot, again the blindfolded girl counting.

Then the mist began to clear, gradually revealing a spectacular mountain scene, the accompanying sound that of a waterfall.

"One!" the girl yelled. At the same moment, a hand reached out and jerked off the blindfold. The girl, Cristiana, looked startled.

Queenie watched as Hannah and Cristiana stood by a waterfall in a sunny clearing, the black blindfold fluttering in Hannah's hands as she gestured angrily. Several children came out from their hiding places.

"Just look at you! Filthy! You were supposed to be home an hour ago. Señor Ballester is here to see you—and you've kept him waiting!"

The scene ended with a shot of the blindfold left on the soft pad of sun-dappled green grass.

Soon after that opening scene, Cristiana (now Nuria) and Miguel Ballester were married in a modest ceremony in Barcelona.

For the next hour and a half Queenie barely moved. Beside her, Freddie chain-smoked. Finally the burial scene she'd watched on video was projected on the screen. However, the close-up of the cross on which dates and Cristiana's full name appeared at the head of the open grave was not the final shot. Here in the rough cut, Freddie ended with a black blindfold resting on blood-splattered snow.

Nathan turned on the lights and began rewinding the film. Nailed by emotion, Queenie didn't stir for several minutes. Then everyone seemed to talk at once. The men gathered around Freddie, the investors clearly pleased. Queenie noticed Muncie move over to Tybalt. Nuria stayed in her seat, smoking and looking glumly at the fireplace.

Finally, Queenie left the room to find Señora Pujol.

The señora stood at the stove scooping beans and sausage from a large pot into an earthenware bowl. She turned and placed the steaming bowl in front of a man Queenie had never seen before.

"*Hola,*" the señora greeted Queenie cheerfully while slicing a thin, crusty loaf. "You hungry? Señor Ballester not feed you enough?" she added with a laugh.

But Queenie was momentarily stunned. She *had* seen the man before. It was the *portero*, Señor Pujol. His trademark beret and blue jacket hung from the back of his wooden chair. His head was now uncovered, and she realized it was shaped just like a light bulb. She shivered, remembering the sensation of being watched last night by the person with the odd-shaped head.

"*Señorina?*"

Her eyes darted to Señora Pujol. "Oh. No, I'm not hungry. I, uh, was wondering if you'd call information in Barcelona for me."

"*Sí. Ahora?*"

"Yes please. Now."

The two women entered the lobby. Outside, Muncie, Carlos, and the two investors were taking their leave of Freddie while Tybalt swayed on the fringe, looking quite drunk. Nuria was absent, had probably gone to her room.

Queenie wrote Michael's full name on a slip of paper, and Señora Pujol made the call, opening the logbook to jot down the information.

Freddie came in and motioned for Queenie to join him in the tea room. "Just leave the number here for me," Queenie said to the señora, then joined Freddie.

Freddie poured two glasses of wine. She accepted his offering as a formality, having no intention of drinking. Clearly, he was in a celebratory mood. She wondered why.

"Cheers!" he said, his face flushed with excitement. "Well, what did you think? I must know!"

For the next few minutes, she detailed her impressions, feeling her own excitement rise, in part due to Freddie's heightened spirits.

Artistically, the film was gorgeous and wonderfully subtle. To an average audience seeking entertainment, the way in which Nuria had been filmed would not likely register on a conscious level. In the Barcelona scenes, the camera was slightly above Nuria and angled down. The country scenes were reversed, with the camera angled slightly up at her—the difference between oppression and empowerment.

Further, by using wardrobe and color, Freddie had created ambiguities in Cristiana's character. Nuria's Barcelona wardrobe consisted of dresses in either off-white or powdery gray or a combination of both, the fabrics soft and liquidy. Also, in the city scenes, he had shot her in diffused light and never straight on, leaving definition nebulous. In Barcelona, her hair was always neatly dressed.

For country scenes, both in the village and at the summer house, Nuria wore trousers and shirts in rough fabrics of earthy browns or stark black. There were more full-face shots with her hair loose.

Altogether, the impression being that in the city, in social settings, there was an artificiality about Cristiana—perhaps a reflection of the bourgeoisie itself. In the country her spirit emerged, whole and guileless.

Cristiana's husband, Miguel, was the opposite. Clearly he lusted after land, in particular that which she'd inherited, but he appeared stiff and uncomfortable when appearing in the few country scenes. For him land had no intrinsic value other than as an object of commerce. Conversely, in Barcelona, his character was commanding and smooth.

Finally Queenie sketched her feelings about the third side of this triangle, Ian Frazier. Though Nuria and the actor playing Miguel Ballester gave good performances, it was Tybalt to whom any accolades might be bestowed. He played the role in an understated way that created so much tension it seeped into all the scenes in which he *didn't* appear. Allegorically, he was Temptation, always being considered even when not indulged in.

"Of course," Queenie said, concluding her analysis, "we're still left with that one gaping hole in the story."

Though well oiled by brandy, wine, and the good words of investors, Freddie tensed slightly. "What hole?"

"Was she the betrayer or the betrayed?"

"Maybe I have been making too much of it," Freddie conceded. "After all, everyone loves the film. Tomorrow we'll shoot the climbing scenes with the girl—what's her name?"

"Isobel."

"Isobel. And then . . . oh yes! I must tell you, Carlos liked what you'd written; finally read it during the drive to the parador. He especially approved of the destruction of the village during the Easter week procession, the people looking quite medieval in their black pointed hoods, flowers crushed beneath their feet—then the chaos and pyrotechnics as the soldiers take them by surprise. He thinks the film should end with the scene you wrote with the wolves surveying the destroyed village and fade out with their plaintive howls."

Queenie swirled her wine, thinking. Clearly this reversal was a personal victory, but she didn't feel good about it. "Freddie," she began cautiously, "those scenes came off the top of my head. I'm grateful your brother approves, but the film's the point here. Your use of the blindfold in the opening scene and at the end works artistically and brings the film around full circle. It's a perfect metaphor. Besides, the village wasn't destroyed until a year later, after Barcelona fell."

"Dammit!" he suddenly spat, "I thought you'd be happy!" Then he wandered off to find someone else to celebrate with, muttering something about "bloody writers."

After returning to her room she kicked off her shoes and changed into more comfortable clothes: jeans and a soft T-shirt which featured singer Chris Isaak on the front.

Now, sitting on her balcony/sanctuary, Queenie puffed a thin, hand-rolled cigarette. From some mountain, a lone wolf howled, the sound more mournful than chilling given her reasonably safe dwelling. Blackness poured down across the country to a fence of lights which, even at this hour, sparkled along the coast. Closer, the familiar emberlike glow rose from the village. She half expected to see the *portero's* misshapen head silhouetted there, and feel his eyes on her— and was glad when she didn't.

On the bare hint of breeze rode a feral scent. Maybe Nat was around.

The call to Michael deBeers had been answered by a machine. She had left a brief message, saying only that she'd call again. After logging the call, she'd flipped through the notebook scanning Digby Patterson's outgoing calls. Before he'd disappeared, he'd made several. Queenie jotted down the numbers, then went on to her room.

Though she hadn't mentioned it to Freddie, she felt strongly that the image of the blindfold transferred itself offscreen as well. No one was really seeing things.

She stubbed out the butt and began to jot down notes. The wolf cried again, closer now, but this time she didn't hear it. She was on the verge of a revelation, as if her own metaphorical blindfold had been momentarily loosened, allowing her a peek. But at what? She concentrated on something heard, something seen, something felt. *Something wrong.*

CHAPTER EIGHTEEN

AT ABOUT ONE A.M., feeling more than a little frightened, Queenie stood gripping the balcony's railing, her body rigid with tension. In the east, the sea and sky formed a seamless gray wall. The air was still, quieted by the mist. She looked up at the moon—it was like looking at a ball of light through a filter smeared with Vaseline.

Again she wondered whom to go to for help. If her judgment proved faulty, she just might get herself killed. She had reduced her choices to Freddie and Tybalt. Though Freddie had hired her to snoop around, Tybalt was physically stronger. Freddie had to be up early for the morning's shoot and probably would not appreciate losing sleep. Tybalt wouldn't be in any of the morning scenes, but how would she explain herself to him if the adventure proved fruitless? And she hoped it *would* be fruitless. Which man was least likely to be a murderer?

Realizing she could spend the entire night debating, she finally just decided on the one she most trusted.

Each room contained a supply of candles and matches, and a flashlight. Obviously, the electricity was as unreliable here as in Barcelona. She flicked on the flashlight. Good, the batteries were working. For backup, she dumped the tallow-colored candles and extra matches into her satchel and left the room.

She noticed a faint glow beneath his door and knocked softly. Tybalt opened it almost instantly. Had he been waiting for someone? Whoever it might be, he saw no need for more than a thigh-length summer kimono. She'd seen quite a lot of him in the love scenes, but propinquity was another matter all together.

"Uh, were you expecting someone?" Then she remembered Muncie.

"One never knows . . ." He laughed. "What can I do for you?"

Let me count the ways . . . "Look, I've got to go down to the location. And I need help."

"Really? What on earth for?"

"Please. Just come with me. Meet me in the kitchen in five minutes."

"The kitchen?" He frowned, then his much too sensuous mouth lifted. "Ah. Is this to be some moonlight picnic?"

"Not quite. And bring your flashlight."

"All right, then. Five minutes."

Isobel had said she stole oranges from the kitchen, which is why Queenie flashed her light around the dark room, aromatic with the scent of onions and garlic, looking for the tunnel entrance. She passed through an archway into the laundry room, and there her efforts were rewarded when her light traced the outline of a rounded wooden door with tarnished hinges at the far end, several feet behind the gaping chute in the ceiling.

"Queenie?" he called out in a stage whisper.

"In here, Tybalt."

"Jesus! What are you doing?"

He'd changed into jeans and a black pullover and appeared both expectant and mystified, suggesting he'd never been here before. But actors were nothing if not accomplished liars.

The door creaked loudly in the gloom. Dank stale air mixed with the warm clean scent of laundry.

"Bloody hell—"

"It's perfectly safe. I think they used to call them monk's passages or something. Come on."

They both had to stoop down, as the passage was built for much shorter people. In the lead, Queenie was alert to anything in the blackness beyond the edge of their lights. At one point, she heard a scratching, then scrambling sound, but she did not stop, as she figured that they were simply disturbing some nocturnal creature. Clearly, though, the tunnel had been used recently, as there were no silky cobwebs. Also, in the hard-packed floor she noted signs of recent passage. Could be, of course, that some of the crew had used the tunnel as a shortcut.

Finally they came to the smooth steps and entered the ruined church, the rubble gray and shadowy in the misty moonlight. They jumped down into the graveyard.

"Watch your step," Queenie cautioned, picking her way among the old crosses and crumbling grave markers.

"You have a macabre sense of romance," Tybalt muttered.

"You ain't seen nothing yet."

Out of the corner of her eye, she saw a flash of white, then heard something in the brush. She quickened her pace.

"Jesus! What was that?" Tybalt said, clearly spooked.

"Shit, I don't know. Maybe a wolf. Does Freddie keep a watch on this place?"

"Tried to enlist some help after the demise of the equipment lorry, but no one wanted to stay here after dark. At the moment, I see their point."

Finally they came to the dusty street and hurried on. Queenie swung her light to the left, where it illuminated the various shops. Toward the end of the street, she came to the hardware store she'd seen earlier that day. She tried the door but it was locked.

She wished she'd brought her lockpicks on this trip—but had hardly thought they'd be needed. Given that the front door was locked, a back door would likely be too. Was B and E a prosecutable crime in a ghost town? But this ghost town was a movie set. She doubted Freddie would have her arrested, though he might well charge her for the glass.

"What the hell," she mumbled, and, using her flashlight, broke the door's pane. The shattering glass sounded doubly loud in the still night.

"Freddie isn't going to like this one bit," Tybalt said.

There was nothing to say. Tybalt was absolutely right.

Reaching in, she unlocked the door and they entered. A drop curtain hid most of the small shop, beyond the merchandise displayed for cinematic purposes. Queenie found two shovels and, keeping one for herself, handed the other to her bewildered-looking companion.

"Why do I have the feeling you haven't brought me here for a kiss and a cuddle?"

"Because you can trust your feelings on this one," she said with a grim smile.

Leaving the shop, they moved to the end of the village and up a slight slope to the fake cemetery. Instead of viewing them from the front, Queenie walked *behind* the crosses, shining her light on each one. Her heart suddenly accelerated when she saw what she'd missed earlier in the day. There was the name, CRISTIANA KAUFMANN BALLESTER, just as it had appeared in the film.

"Queenie! You must tell me what's going on!"

"Look, Tybalt!" She shone her light on the marker. "You see, it's backward!"

Stepping around to the front, Queenie used the shovel to roughly outline the dimensions of the grave. Finally, she looked at his handsome face. "Tybalt," she said softly, "it's time to go to work."

It was after three when they finished, both filthy, sweating, and shirtless. He'd appraised her momentarily when she too threw off her T-shirt. But he'd quickly resumed digging, sex now far from his mind. A rivulet of dirty sweat trickled between her breasts. Her chest was heaving, as was his, from exertion and now the excitement that comes of horror and fear.

The smell, grave gas from rotting flesh, revolted both of them.

"Holy Jesus. What should we do?" he asked.

"I'll stay here. You go back to the parador. Call the police," she said, still gripping the shovel, barely aware of the pain in her hands.

"You can't stay here alone."

1 5 3

"Why not? I'm certainly not afraid of whatever's in that coffin. But if there're wolves around, they might try and get at it. The scene shouldn't be disturbed any more than necessary." Her voice was surprisingly calm and steady.

He started to move away, then changed his mind and moved up and put his arms around her. A moment of truth had arrived, the test of her judgment of Tybalt. If he meant to hurt her, now would be the time.

"Dear God," he whispered in her ear. "Who is it?"

She pulled away and looked up into sad but knowing eyes. He really didn't have to ask. Gently, he leaned down and kissed her. She felt something ignite, the fuse attached to a powerful explosive. His tongue prodded, then withdrew. He stepped back.

"Jesus," he said breathlessly. "I don't know what came over me."

They stared at each other sharing a certain disbelief, then Queenie said, "It's all right. The proximity to death draws the living together, for comfort mainly."

"I'd best get going." He picked up his shirt.

She nodded, then slipped on her T-shirt. "Take the tunnel. I know you don't like it, but it's faster."

Then, instead of putting on his pullover he gave it to her. "It's warmer than yours. I'll be back soon as I can."

"Here," she said and handed him her flashlight. Then she took two candles from her satchel and gave him one, along with some matches. "Just in case," she added, and lit a candle for herself.

She watched his light bob in the darkness until it disappeared behind the facade of the church. Well, scratch one suspect. Of course she should have realized he had no intention of harming her when they'd hit something solid, the lid in fact—a stench rising—and he'd insisted she get out of the grave. Chivalry, perhaps, and the urge to shield her from possible unpleasantness.

The candle glowed, the flame shivering slightly in the still air. Queenie stood sentry over the open grave, shovel in hand should she have to chase off any creature drawn by the smell of death, and waited for someone to pry the lid from the coffin. Perversely, the thought occurred to her that they just might have found Señora Pujol's missing sheet.

CHAPTER NINETEEN

"Una mujer con dos sepulturas . . ."

QUEENIE AND TYBALT drank coffee on the veranda, excused for the moment from the chaos within the parador. A slim volume of poetry lay open in his lap. He'd just read aloud one line, then lowered the book, no doubt unable to completely put the current situation from mind.

He'd returned to the grave site after rousing the local policeman, who in turn alerted the big guns in Gerona. Around five A.M., a small crowd of police had assembled and the coffin was hoisted out of its resting place.

Digby Patterson had been stabbed in the heart; the sheet his body had been wrapped in was blood-caked and putrid. A rope tied his corpse in a neat package. A local cop went into the brush and puked. Tybalt did the same after identifying the body. The Gerona authorities were clearly more accustomed to such sights and smells.

An English-speaking detective from Gerona questioned Queenie at the grave site. Afterward he questioned Tybalt then drove them back to the parador, where preparations were just getting underway for the morning's shoot. Freddie had planned to rehearse with Nuria and Isobel, then film the climbing scenes day for night. Not today.

Queenie had chosen to stay on the veranda, as much to keep out of the way while her room was being searched as to intercept Isobel. She'd sent the girl back home, trying to smooth Isobel's obvious disappointment with reassuring clichés such as "The show must go on"—but later. Indeed, that would depend on the authorities.

Carlos Ballester had pulled into the parking lot while Queenie talked to Isobel, his Rolls-Royce standing out like a royal carriage among the lotful of proletarian police vehicles. He had strode purposefully into the parador. If anyone could keep the film from shutting down, it was Don Carlos. For the moment, she actually liked him.

And so now, at nearly eight o'clock, Queenie refilled their coffee cups. Tybalt appeared shell-shocked.

"May I see the book?" she asked.

Without looking at her, he passed it over.

"'*Una mujer con dos sepulturas*,'" she repeated. "A woman with two . . ."

"Graves," Tybalt translated flatly. Then he sighed deeply. "I tried to convince Digs and Freddie that I should spout some of this stuff every now and again."

"Might provide interesting dialogue say, during a love scene."

Tybalt cast her a derisive look. "Discussing a woman with two graves while making love? Ian Frazier was no Andrew Marvell—this is hardly *To a Coy Mistress*."

"But you just said you tried—"

"Never mind what I just said," he retorted irritably.

" '*Una en la tierra y una en mi corazón partido,*' " Queenie continued. " 'One in the earth and one in my' . . . what?"

"Broken heart." He snatched the book out of her hand. "I shouldn't have brought this down. Hardly comforting stuff." He tossed the book onto the table.

A shroud of gloom descended on them, created largely from Tybalt's mood. While he had sought out her company, she didn't want to brood with him. Her second job was now in operation. She wondered what clues might exist in Barcelona. She couldn't go anywhere until the cops released her, but doubted her detention would be long since she hadn't been in the country when Patterson was murdered. The state of his body indicated he'd been in the ground at least a week. All she'd done was find him—in itself, of course, fodder for some suspicion.

Tybalt suddenly jumped out of his chair, returning a moment later with a bottle of Osborne brandy—not the satiny stuff she'd drunk in the elevator with Michael deBeers, but a more common vintage. He tossed his coffee out on the grass and refilled his cup with the amber beverage. She shook her head when he offered her the bottle. After a couple swallows, he seemed to loosen up.

"How did you know?" he said, ripping into the silence.

"Know?"

"Where to find Digs. How did you know?"

"In the rough cut we screened, the grave wasn't filled in. Yesterday when I visited the site, it was. I figured after the scene was shot the site had probably been ignored. No reason to go back there except to reshoot. Quite possibly I wouldn't have thought much about it except for the cross. Anyway, why would it have been turned around? Especially if no one had been back to the site."

"I mean, why would you even think of it?"

"Curiosity," she said, not lying, just not telling the complete truth. "I wanted to know what happened to Patterson. As I've said more than once, if he showed up, I'd be out of a job." Then she more or less took up where they'd left off in the school kitchen when they first met.

"Tell me about the last time you saw him."

"It was Friday a week. We knocked off for the day around four. Freddie flew back with the dailies to Barcelona. I joined Digs and Nuria for a few bevies at the local pub. Nat came in and asked if anyone wanted to ride back to the city with him. Stupid question. He was taking the Jag. He might have gotten a more positive response if he hadn't included the 'with him' bit. Anyway, he had a beer and took off on his own."

"What time?"

"Around six. I remember because the pub starts to fill up about that time and outside it gets dead quiet. We were on the back terrace.

"I was planning to leave in the morning. Digs said he was staying, as he preferred the quiet of the country to finish up. We, of course, were all curious as to how he was writing the ending but he refused to tell us. I hoped after more wine, he might loosen up.

"Nuria left shortly before seven to take the coach with the crew back to Barcelona. So Digs and I spent the evening getting pleasantly sloshed. And, I might add, he spoke no more of the script. We argued sport and politics until about midnight. Then went back to our rooms.

159

"As you know, my room is directly beneath his—yours—but in my Morphean state, I heard nothing."

"How drunk was he when you left him?"

"Pretty bloody drunk."

"In your opinion, what happened after you left him?"

"I'm an actor. I have no opinions."

She nearly choked on her coffee.

"Tell me," he continued, "does this curiosity of yours tell you anything about the killer?"

"As a matter of fact, yes."

He turned and looked at her sharply. "Well?"

"Whoever did it isn't entirely heartless."

"What? The man was bloody-well stabbed to death!"

"That's the point, Tybalt. Patterson could have been buried alive."

CHAPTER TWENTY

TRUE ENOUGH, SOMEONE had wanted Patterson dead and out of the way. Suffering had nothing to do with intent. Otherwise, why bother stabbing the poor bastard?

"That's revolting!" A man of surprisingly tender sensibilities, Tybalt grabbed the brandy and stalked off to commiserate with the trees.

As cold-blooded as the observation sounded, still, Queenie believed it to be true. Alone for the moment, she reconstructed the crime, as it may have happened, using what she'd heard and seen so far.

A hard and heavy drinker, Patterson had returned to his room around midnight last Friday. Fully clothed, he got into bed and passed out. His killer had been waiting in the room, maybe in the wardrobe. While Patterson slept, the killer tossed all of his clothes, toiletries, and papers into a bag and sent it down the laundry chute. Next he wrapped Patterson in a sheet taken from Señora Pujol's linen supplies, tying the human bundle with rope. He straightened the top sheet and cover to make it appear that Patterson had made the bed before leaving the parador. Then he sent Patterson's body down the chute, and followed thereafter.

The rest was easy enough. He simply dragged the body down the tunnel and through the ghost town to the open grave, dumped it into the coffin, and, before nailing down the lid, stabbed the writer in the heart.

At one point he must have put the cross to one side, or possibly it had fallen over or into the grave while he was maneuvering the body into position. Finally, he shoveled in the earth heaped on either side, repositioned the cross, and took off with the bag of Patterson's personal effects, and the murder weapon, which he later disposed of.

Acquiring the shovel, hammer, and nails would have presented no problem, as all the tools would be available at the location. As for gaining access to Patterson's room, well, from what Queenie had seen, that would not be difficult. The room keys were behind the reception desk along with the telephone logbook. Since Señora Pujol had stated that no keys were missing, Queenie imagined that the killer had borrowed a key from reception, unlocked Patterson's door, then returned the key. Finally, he had entered the room, locked it from the inside, and waited.

Whoever killed Patterson had to have been familiar enough with the parador to know where the linens were kept, had to know about the chute in Patterson's room, and about the monk's passage. But that could be just about anyone working on the film, as they'd lived there on and off for a couple months.

She was just beginning to consider the weapon when Freddie plopped down beside her, grasping a cup of coffee with the scent and appearance of sludge. No acorns had gone into that brew. He looked like someone who had just ridden in with the Four Horsemen of the Apocalypse.

"I honestly never imagined it would come to this," he remarked, a noticeable tremor in his voice. "I mean it, Q, find the villain who did this, and anything I can give is yours."

"I'll remember that, Freddie. You haven't told the police or your brother about me, then?"

"No. Carlos wouldn't be pleased to know I'd resorted to hiring a detective, especially without his knowledge. As for the police, it's my impression they don't get on with members of your profession. That could be doubly troublesome here, in that you're a foreigner. I also know the police must plod within certain parameters. Their investigation could take weeks . . . even months, which I don't have if I want to resolve the question of Cristiana's betrayal—at least on film."

This man could certainly vacillate. "Last night you seemed quite pleased with the film more or less as is. I got the impression you'd decided the betrayal factor was superfluous."

"Yes, well. When the wine is in, the wit is out, as they say. Besides, getting caught up in the investors' praise, I quite forgot original intent."

With jerky movements he offered her a cigarette, and when she declined, lit one for himself, inhaling deeply.

"For the moment, the location is off limits. I'm afraid your room is as well. You're free, though, seeing as how you've only been in the country a few days. The rest of us are under a sort of house arrest.

"Carlos is trying to secure permission to shoot the mountain scenes, though I doubt that will happen until things quiet down a bit. We're all under suspicion and they don't want anyone deciding to run over the border."

"Life imitating art?"

He smiled ruefully. "As for me, I'll be busy enough dealing with the paparazzi. To be honest, the publicity won't do us any harm, that is, if I handle things properly. I've been thinking, it might be best if you returned to Barcelona."

"You'll keep me abreast of any developments here?"

"Of course. Now, I'll see about collecting your things."

She handed him her satchel. "Everything goes in here."

"Right then," he said and stood up. He started to leave, then stopped as Carlos approached carrying a small can of film.

"In going over your room the police found this in the back of your wardrobe," Carlos said in a voice unmistakably angry. "Have I paid for something I don't know about?"

Freddie took the can and stuck it under his arm. "It's only outtakes I wanted put aside."

"Then why hide it?"

The conversation faded as the two men entered the parador. Queenie considered how stressful it must be for Freddie when his brother was around. Certainly no love existed between the two men. Worst of all, though, was working with an interfering producer who lacked filmmaking experience.

Queenie went to refill her coffee from the nearby urn. Tybalt suddenly appeared beside her, so close she could smell the brandy on his breath.

"We'd best go inside," he said softly and took her by the arm.

Her heart leaped when she saw the reason for his concern.

A group of people, a few of whom she recognized as locals, stood silently staring at them from the other side of the parking lot. She'd neither seen nor heard their approach but then she hadn't been looking in that direction.

Someone threw a rock, smashing a window in front of them. She and Tybalt began to run along the veranda, their feet crunching broken glass. Hot coffee sloshed on her hand. She dropped the cup as more rocks whizzed by. Tybalt cried out, then tucked her close. At the same moment one of the police cars burst into flames. The two stumbled through the doorway as a hail of sharp stones hit windows, dislodged plaster, and skittered across the lobby floor.

Queenie would remember the next few minutes primarily for the screams and shouts of the eerie mob and the answering blasts when Señor Pujol suddenly dashed through the lobby with a shotgun, opening fire before he'd even gotten out the door. Cops came tearing down the stairs. Queenie and Tybalt jumped into the tea room to avoid being trampled, and slammed the door. There was a deafening explosion, then suddenly a car door shot through the window, crashing into the tiled fireplace. For a split second, the spinning shards seemed to hang in the sunlight and, bursting with color, changed the room into a deadly kaleidoscope. Using his body as a shield, Tybalt slammed Queenie against the door as shattered glass rained down on his head and back. She could barely distinguish his thundering heartbeat from her own. Their sweat and fear joined as one.

Another explosion reverberated through the parador. Tybalt pressed harder. Pain shot up Queenie's back as the doorknob knuckled her spine. They were much too close to the parking lot.

"Holy Mother! We can't stay here," she cried, pushing

him away. Queenie threw open the door and they dashed through the smoky lobby, past the reception desk toward the kitchen. Señora Pujol flew past them and grabbed the phone. They could hear her screaming something in Catalan.

In the kitchen, Queenie quickly turned off all the gas burners on the stove, where Señora Pujol had left food cooking. Detectives who'd been in the laundry room ran through the kitchen, ignoring the pair.

"Christ Almighty," Tybalt moaned and sank into a chair by the table. Queenie found a bowl and filled it with hot water, then grabbed a clean dish towel. Pushing aside a cutting board laden with chopped tomatoes, she set the bowl down and began mopping Tybalt's bloody face.

A rock had caught him just above his left eye at the hairline. He'd need stitches. Tiny shards of glass glistened in his black hair, across his shoulders and down his back.

They stepped out the back door for a moment to brush and shake off the small bits of glass. Back in the kitchen, Queenie made a small ice pack to stop the blood flow. He held it in place while she cracked an egg. Taking the ice pack from him, she cleaned and dried the area as best she could, then daubed lightly with egg white. When dry, the albumen would seal the wound.

"Now, if you can keep a straight face, that should hold until medics arrive."

"Can't see myself laughing anytime soon."

Queenie washed and dried her hands, then peeked into the lobby. There was little noise and activity in the parador itself, but she could still hear shouts and movement in the distance, and thought she heard a siren.

"Probably the local chapter of the ETA," Tybalt said.

Queenie turned, but kept an eye on the lobby. "What would they have to do with us?"

"A large gathering of authorities tends to turn them rather queer; probably couldn't resist all those police cars. And if we get in the way, that's our bad luck . . . Christ. There's more to these quaint villages than one thinks."

She remembered the blindfold as metaphor and silently agreed.

Along with reinforcements and ambulances came the local media. Amazingly, no one had died—at least, not in the parking lot. Two police cars were totaled; most other vehicles had sustained some damage. Freddie's Jag had suffered a few dents from falling debris, but luckily nothing to impair drive-ability.

Minor hysteria prevailed for the next couple of hours. From Señora Pujol and others, Queenie and Tybalt managed to piece together the story. Tybalt had figured correctly.

News of the police presence at the parador had spread quickly. Seeing an opportunity for mischief, Basque terrorists—the ETA—had struck then vanished. The locals, of course, professed to know nothing. The few who'd come up to the parador said they'd just been curious to see what was going on. Those who'd been detained were released. No arrests were made.

Freddie brought Queenie her satchel, now packed with her clothes, notes, and the script.

"They're keeping the typewriter, since it belonged to Digs." He gave her his car keys and told her maps were in the glove box. He urged her to slip away at her earliest convenience, then went off with a police spokesman to deal with the press. At the moment, the story of the attack overshadowed the murder. A medical crew mended and bandaged Tybalt, who seemed to be the only person with injuries, and those superficial.

While Señora Pujol assembled a cleanup crew and supervised repairs, Tybalt graciously finished luncheon preparations. He and Queenie set up a buffet in the kitchen, then took their own plates outside as storm clouds skittered across the mountains. The excitement had washed away Queenie's fatigue, and she devoured her food.

Too dazed for conversation, they sat quietly watching the advance of the threatening clouds, and smoked after-meal cigarettes.

But the peace was short-lived. They heard a shout, then Freddie and two policeman trotted toward them. One policeman carried the soft leather bag Queenie recognized from her first meeting with Tybalt. Freddie looked like someone lost in a maze.

"Oh no," Queenie moaned, knowing what was about to happen.

CHAPTER TWENTY-ONE

THE FOUNDATION OF Spanish law is the Napoleonic te-
net: guilty until proven innocent. They might not be seeing
Tybalt for some time—offscreen or on.

Wasting no time, the police had gotten the dimensions of
Digby's fatal wound and matched them with those of Tybalt's bayonet right there in the leather bag in his room. The
police took Tybalt into custody, adding yet another sensational tale to the apocrypha surrounding his life.

For a moment, Queenie was alone. An explosive day all
around, she reflected, her thoughts scored by a dark, rum-
bling sky. And in that opaque and silvery light, colors
seemed painfully vivid. Spring's fragile vulnerability had
transmogrified, its beauty vibrating in a dimension of evil.
Grass and flowers seemed to be growing in a crust of dried
blood.

If Tybalt's bayonet really was the murder weapon, then it had to have been returned to his room while he slept. Unless Tybalt himself had simply put it back in his bag believing that no one would ever discover the body.

Freddie returned after a few minutes. The crowds still remained at the front of the parador, no doubt devouring the sight of Tybalt St. Germain between his stoic captors.

"Such a bloody senseless act!"

"Patterson's murder?" she asked, somewhat bemused.

"What the hell else would I be talking about?" Freddie snapped angrily, the question obviously rhetorical.

"Well, two police cars exploded in the parking lot," Queenie reminded him.

"Do you think Tybalt did it?" he went on.

"I don't know."

"You dug up the bloody body with him; you've been talking to him."

"Actors lie on demand," she said, her emotions beginning to poke sharp spikes through a wall about as tough as the skin on hot milk. She considered reminding him that the situation was quite new to her, that even great detectives don't possess some inner oracle that instantly identifies the guilty. But that would have been self-defense and a waste of time. Instead she asked, "What about the last time you saw Patterson alive?"

"I told you before."

"Tell me again. You might have seen or heard something helpful."

He ignored her, emotion clouding his objectivity. "Carlos is furious; thinks it morally unthinkable to continue producing a movie with a murderer playing the male lead. Christ.

Unless new evidence comes up proving Tybalt's innocence, he's considering cutting off the money—which means we'll be booted out of the parador, the equipment'll be returned to the hire firm—"

"Keep your head, Freddie," Queenie interrupted.

Certainly, Freddie could find another actor and reshoot Ian's scenes. But another *bankable* actor? That would be dependent on sheer luck, not something investors counted on. And it would be expensive. Most likely, Carlos would settle something with the insurance company, write off the loss, and doom what was already in the can to some dark, dusty vault.

"Now tell me *again* about the last time you saw Patterson—not only Tybalt's fate but the *film's* might depend on it." Mention of the film prodded his memory.

"We spoke in his room just before I caught the courier flight to Barcelona—Friday around two P.M. He hadn't joined us for lunch. I remember a pot of tea on the desk. He'd used a pair of underpants as a cozy."

"What was his mood?"

"Preoccupied. Said we may have to reshoot a part of the last ten minutes."

"But he didn't say specifically the ending, the burial scene?"

"No. He seemed a bit put out by the interruption. Didn't offer me tea. Just as well."

She wondered if he was thinking of the unusual cozy. "Did he often have people in his room?"

"Quite the opposite. He hated interruptions."

"When we arrived you said Nathan wanted to stay in Patterson's room. How did he know what it was like?"

"Hmm. Well, it's unlikely Digs would have invited him in for tea."

The temperature continued to drop. Freddie studied the sky for a moment; even in his short-sleeved shirt he seemed unaware of the chilling air. Noticing his fresh, clean clothes served to remind Queenie of her own appearance. Dirt from the grave dusted her clothing and hair. She realized she was still wearing Tybalt's pullover on top of her T-shirt. Absently she rubbed the soft wool.

"When I first met you, you told me the computer had 'blown up.' Did that happen here at the parador?"

"Happened several weeks ago. At the Barcelona flat. It's in the shop, unlikely to be repaired for another month."

"So, Patterson was using the typewriter when you last saw him."

He seemed to jump aboard her train of thought. "Of course!"

"Which means someone took the typewriter back to Barcelona, no doubt to make it appear that Patterson had returned to the city. Also, I noticed a newspaper there with last Monday's date. Someone planted those items. And that someone had to have keys to the apartment."

At that moment, Carlos appeared in the kitchen doorway and called to Freddie, who jumped up and started back toward the parador.

"Look, we still have one chance."

"Oh?" He didn't stop, his slumped shoulders telling her he'd once again accepted the burden of defeat.

"Would you please listen?"

He stopped and stared at her. In the eerie light his skin looked greasy gray, reminding her of the Tin Man.

"We prove Tybalt didn't kill Patterson."

"How soon? Carlos is an impatient man. I'm afraid you'd have to work round the clock." Then he hurried off.

She watched him disappear inside the parador. Nathan had keys to the apartment, but so did Freddie.

"I'm not tired," she muttered.

"You're a fool, Davilov," Queenie said out loud, her hands still gripping the wheel of Freddie's Jaguar. She was too wired to cry and too scared to laugh. Finally, she pried one hand loose and shut off the engine. Then the other hand came loose and she rested her head against the seat while breathing damp air from the open window. A cat cried out in loneliness. Thunder bawled a warning that more was to come.

The sudden spring storm had provided unwelcome company on the drive to Barcelona. She had never steered on the passenger side—though her feet had often stomped imaginary brake pedals while she rode with someone else—and she didn't have an international driver's permit. Freddie's assurance that as long as she had a driver's license, she'd be okay, hadn't been of much comfort. Still, she'd made it to the city and up onto the sidewalk several yards from the apartment house. Despite the nerve-wracking fear that she'd be pulled over for some minor infraction, or that due to a wrong turn she'd end up in France, her deepest concern was in the heart. She'd fallen in love . . . or into something.

Again she cursed herself, feeling all the symptoms: vulnerability, yearning, concern for Tybalt's well-being, a sexual ache, guilt for betraying Dick, uncertainty, the terrible thought that her emotions were not shared—and that if they were, it was possibly by a cold-blooded murderer!

Up ahead, two figures left Carmella's bar. As they approached, Queenie saw a woman walking slightly ahead of a man. Abruptly, the woman strutted across the street. Their voices carried in the stillness. Though Queenie couldn't understand the rapid Spanish, anger in the woman's voice was obvious. Outside the shadows of the *panadería*, the woman stopped and spun around to face the man. Their voices lowered, and they began the ageless dance, beginning with the man moving forward, the woman stepping backward. They both stopped for a moment. Then the woman moved forward and the man took a step backward. Finally, they embraced, intertwined as one lumpy shape that sank into the shadows and out of sight.

Queenie sat up. Foolish or not, her feelings had to be corralled. She needed that energy to fuel, not cloud the investigation. Suddenly she realized that Digby Patterson and the script were one, entangled just like the two people coupling in the darkness of the bakery. Solve the riddle of the script and she'd have his killer.

She exited and locked the car then let herself into the building. The elevator looked innocent enough, but she chose the stairs, unwilling to risk a night spent in the cab.

She made the climb slowly but steadily, breathing in through her nose and exhaling through her mouth. The short time in the mountains had improved her stamina, though not enough to keep leg muscles from quivering and chest from heaving. At least she hadn't crawled the last few flights.

She let herself into the apartment, and her thoughts went back to Digby. His was no senseless killing—Digby Patterson had been silenced.

One more thing, she reminded herself: Anyone attempting to resurrect his voice will likely be targeted for murder as well.

To nix that sobering thought, she took a liter of wine from the refrigerator and poured a glass. In the living room, she found the telephone beside the sofa, pulled from her satchel the note with Michael DeBeers's phone number, and dialed. Beside the telephone was a pamphlet. She picked it up and studied it while waiting for her call to be answered.

A black-and-white photograph dominating the cover featured a benign-looking priest wearing glasses and stooping slightly to clutch the hands of a man in a wheelchair. In the background two women looked on. At the bottom was the declaration: "The Servant of God JOSEMARIA ESCRIVA DE BALAGUER, Founder of Opus Dei."

"*Dígame.*"

"Michael. It's Queenie Davilov."

"Great! I've been hoping you'd call."

"Are you free for guide-duty tomorrow?"

"Sure. Where do you want to go?"

"Just be at the apartment at eight. That's A.M., Michael."

He laughed. "Not to worry. Shall I buzz or come on up? I still have my keys."

"Come on up, then."

After ringing off, from memory she called Dick's number in L.A., hoping his voice would squelch her suddenly combustible feelings for Tybalt.

"Dick!" she exclaimed when he answered on the second ring. She jerked forward, causing the pamphlet to fall to the floor.

"Q-*chan*," he said provocatively. "How goes the battle?"

She didn't feel like explaining and, anyway, it was his

voice she wanted to hear. After a perfunctory answer, she asked about the book he was writing on Yakuza, the Japanese mafia.

"Can't work worth shit," he replied. "I don't know what it is, spring maybe, but lately the UCLA sorority houses seem to have annexed this house."

After the earthquake, a pair of former college buddies had offered Dick the spare room in a house they were renting. Like Queenie, he'd stayed on rather than going through the hassle of looking for a place.

Two weeks ago they'd agreed not to see each other while he finished the second draft of his manuscript—something about channeling his sexual tension into writing. But just hearing that other women were in close proximity gave her a twinge of jealousy.

"Anyway, I'm taking a breather."

"Wish I was there to breathe with you."

He laughed. "Actually, I'm thinking about heading out to my mother's place. After your job's done, maybe we could meet."

Her heart rate shot up dangerously. Calm down, Davilov, she told herself. But his voice had woven its spell; the images it projected created a certain pleasurable distress.

"I don't know when I'll be finished here, but give me the number. At least I could call and see if you're there."

They spoke for another minute or two, then she hung up, absently staring at the number scribbled in her address book. For Dick to consider a trip to his mother's place implied something more than an inability to work at home. While his voice hadn't betrayed any emotion, the nature of his book—an exposé of the machinations of Yakuza in American business—certainly suggested that things might be a little hot for him. Add to the equation the fact that his mother's place wasn't just down the road but in *Ireland*, and it seemed justifiable to conclude that he might be in some danger. But Dick was a sensible, cautious man, and while she felt some apprehension, she didn't worry about him.

She bent down to retrieve the pamphlet that had fallen from her lap and noticed a piece of paper had slipped from the pages. On it was written, "Child of the Time." She flipped it over, but there was nothing else. It seemed vaguely familiar—and old movie title?

Slightly yellowed, the pamphlet looked to be a permanent fixture beside the telephone. She put it and the piece of paper back on the shelf, then called longtime friend and current housemate Josephine Werlanda Burroughs.

For the six years Queenie had known her, Joey had chosen house-sitting as the cheapest means to keep a roof over her head. A believer in impermanence, Joey had not bothered to rent or buy even when her career as a gossip columnist escalated, shooting her into the precipitous aerie of sudden financial and social mobility. Though she now had her own column in *World Abuzz*, she continued house-sitting, shunning obscene mortgages and/or rents.

"Joey Burroughs."

"Joey, it's Q."

"Got a call on another line."

Queenie had half expected Joey to immediately milk her for details of the film and its stars for possible inclusion in her column.

"Can you hold?"

"Yeah, but—"

Show tunes began playing on the line. Absently, Queenie picked up the piece of paper with "Child of the Time" written on it. Out loud, she repeated the words, and while doing so, remembered the children's book she'd seen in the parador.

CHAPTER TWENTY-TWO

WHEN JOEY CAME back on the line, Queenie quickly told her of Patterson's murder and Tybalt's subsequent detention. She asked Joey to check her files for any background information on both the writer and the actor, as well as on Freddie, Nathan, and Nuria.

"Tybalt St. Germain suspected of murdering Digby Patterson?" Joey repeated incredulously. "I don't believe this! Jesus, Davilov, this is hot! How do I get in touch with you?"

As Queenie gave her the phone number, she realized she didn't know the proper address—not that it mattered. "There's no machine here. So, if there's no answer keep trying."

"One more thing. Would you mind if I borrowed Dick tomorrow night?"

Queenie tensed. "What's up?"

Joey rattled off the name of a well-known director she'd been seeing. ". . . left for New York yesterday. With his wife. Anyway, there's this big party at Fox and I don't want to go alone."

"Why Dick? You've got a stable full of escorts."

"Queenie! Dick's gorgeous; everyone will think I'm dating Keanu Reeves . . . including Bob," she said. Clearly Joey wanted to make her married lover jealous. Queenie felt a little easier.

"So, what if Reeves shows up?"

"Q, you always complicate things."

"Well, I'm not Dick's social secretary. Ask him."

There was a pause. "I already did."

"And?"

"He said yes."

After ringing off, Queenie rolled a cigarette, trying not to picture Joey and Dick together. She wondered why he'd not mentioned the date. But maybe he simply didn't think it was important.

Compulsively, she continued rolling cigarettes until she had a small stack. If and when she gave up smoking, she doubted she'd ever quit rolling. The act centered her mind, allowing her to compartmentalize specific problems. She often used her computer for the same purpose—but no such technology was available now.

Ignoring the light rain, she stood on the terrace, half-aware of the watery lights coming on in the surrounding buildings, where potted palms and forgotten laundry fluttered in the cooling evening breeze. From somewhere below, the sound of an argument filtered up, followed by distant high-pitched blasts from a car's security system.

Barely aware of outside noise, she began to assemble pieces as if, together, she and Dick were a jigsaw puzzle, beginning with the two photographs framed in silver and destroyed in the earthquake. She remembered the unsmiling, aristocratic Japanese man dressed in formal riding gear astride a handsome Tennessee walker, with Meiji Palace a blur in the background. The second photograph featured Dick's mother, a dark-haired, blue-eyed beauty with a dimpled smile, less formally attired in muddy Wellington boots, khaki jodhpurs, and a cable-knit sweater, her hand on the bridle of a dapple gray she stood beside, the rolling green fields of Ireland her backdrop.

Both former Olympic equestrians, Dick's parents owned stud farms in Virginia and County Cork, Ireland, and were patrons of such renowned stables as Stoneridge in Ontario, Canada.

Queenie's mother, too, raised horses, but her image was preserved in a rough-edged snapshot, the red clay of Oklahoma beneath her dusty cowboy boots, her denim work shirt and overalls faded and worn. A long black braid hung from beneath a battered cowboy hat—an Australian Akubra, as Queenie recalled, a gift from some long-ago admirer. L.J. squatted beside a sturdy chestnut quarter horse, one of whose forelegs rested on her thigh as she examined the shoe. There were no silver frames for Lillian Jeanette Davilov, who ventured no farther than Arkansas and Texas to buy and sell stock. And no man to complete the picture.

Queenie lit a second cigarette. While the venues of their childhoods had been similar, economics formed a deep rift between Queenie and Dick. Oddly they'd emerged on their separate sides as writers, their separate struggles bridging the gap between them, though not with something as elegantly engineered as the Golden Gate. No, something more primitive, a rope bridge maybe. Before it had been condemned, she'd lived at the St. Albans in Hollywood because it was all she could afford. Dick's reason for choosing such rough digs had come from the romantic notion of the struggling artist; he had been determined to live on the relatively small sum advanced by the publisher of his book on Yakuza. Even so, he still had a comfortable monetary cushion to fall back on should reality impose on idealism.

Suddenly Queenie felt swallowed by a consuming loneliness, one with no beginning and no end. Never a prison with definable boundaries, loneliness was as vast as it was nebulous, and expanded with each hollow cry. But it also provided escape into self-absorption—and this was no time for brooding. What she, like Dick, needed was a breather, and some mindless activity.

Abruptly, she went back inside and made another call, then took a much-needed shower.

The rain had changed into a gluey mist which both muted and increased sound. Michael deBeers's match flared, to Queenie's ears popping like a gunshot. She jumped. He put a hand on her arm as he lit the cigarette. She watched the fog ingest the exhaled stream of smoke, as if both were living things, a big fish eating a little one.

Without hesitation, Michael had responded to her call, and upon arrival, suggested a walk through Putxet, the park near the apartment. He pointed out the century plant, tall as a flagpole, which he said bloomed once every hundred years.

It wasn't blooming now. But there were red calla lilies and his own blossoming comfort.

After the park, he put her in his car and gave her a mini-tour of the city. On pavement slick with the sweat of night, he walked her around Gaudí's Sagrada Familia, closed now and bordered by far less imaginative architecture. The eight spires reminded her of Chinese finger adornments used to protect long, yellow nails. He drove her past Parc Güell and a couple other somewhat wavy gray apartment buildings designed by Gaudí. Altogether, Gaudí's style brought to mind Simon Rodia's Tower of Watts in L.A., a cement-coated steel skeleton decorated with shells, glass, and broken plates.

He parked off the Plaça de Cataluña and walked her down to the Barrio Gótico, past stands of leather-clad male and female hookers, and bought her wine and showed her pocked and stained walls where people had been blindfolded and shot during the civil war.

Wary of seeming too familiar, he lightly held her arm while they walked up the Ramblas, where the newspaper kiosks, the flower and bird stalls were quiet now, and the pastel street art dissolved beneath their feet. Music and laughter lurched from the neighboring bars and restaurants.

"Sometimes I walk here at night and imagine the earth beneath the pavement swelling with the blood of millennia. I think the city has a dangerous sophistication that can bewitch people."

While his commentary was, at times, odd, she was grateful for the shift in focus. Her sexual and emotional anxiety were now on the wane.

They returned to his car. He produced his flask of brandy and politely lit her cigarette.

"What I love about Barcelona, though, is that one can see the past and future in an adjusted present, existing like a well-matched couple respectful of each other's differences."

Then, while she sipped brandy, he drove her home. The interlude, for all its touristy ordinariness, had calmed her.

Shutting off the engine, he turned to her and said, "I know it's not eight A.M. yet, but I am here."

"You must have a thousand girlfriends."

The scar by his mouth dissolved into a dimple. "From what I know about Americans, you—they—always expect something beyond friendship or generosity. All I can say is, I'll stay with you and I don't expect any, uh, reward. Of course, if you can get me a job in the movies, I wouldn't decline the offer."

Feeling reassured by his presence, she slept soundly and awoke refreshed the next morning. She joined Michael around eight on the terrace, where he had thoughtfully provided coffee and croissants.

"You must have ten *thousand* girlfriends," she remarked while they breakfasted to the sound of thunking tennis balls. He'd spent the night in the adjoining bedroom, which, in fact, had once been his own. He looked good as new despite the fact that they'd stayed up talking until after two A.M.

Maybe it was the wine or the sudden case of loneliness, but she'd taken him into her confidence—not all the way, of course. At first he'd been astonished when she admitted to being a private investigator, but the excitement of a murder investigation had sucked him in. He proved the fact when he said:

"About an hour ago, I went down to the first-floor apartment in this stack and told the man who lives there that I'd dropped some papers down the lightwell and would he mind if I retrieved them. I filled a bag and left it in the study." He shrugged. "Who knows? Might be a clue there."

"Excellent," Queenie said, feeling justified in making him her confederate. "Now, are there any English-language libraries in the city?" she asked, recalling Patterson's "secret" of success.

"That's easy, the North American Institute and the British Institute. You'll probably want to go to the British Institute first, since Digby Patterson was British. But they don't open until ten."

"I've got some calls to make."

"Okay. Frankly, I'd like to go home and change. How about I meet you back here in say, two hours?"

"Fine."

When he left, she took the breakfast things into the kitchen, then telephoned the parador. She was glad that Freddie was easy to find.

"Any news?"

"Only that Tybalt's bayonet has been determined to be the murder weapon. And he's been officially charged. Which means the rest of us are no longer being detained. But so what? We'll all be scattered to the wind anyway."

"How are you?"

"Well, quite simply I am getting pissed. In the morning they shall pour me out of the parador."

"What about shooting the scenes with Isobel?"

"I do envy your optimism, Q. Unthinkable for me, I'm afraid."

"Have you talked to Tybalt?" She made a special effort to keep the emotion out of her voice.

"No. And frankly, I could care less if I ever do again." There was a pause, then he said, "Oh, by the way, be prepared to vacate the flat."

"Why?"

"Dear God, girl, I told you, Carlos owns it!"

CHAPTER TWENTY-THREE

SHE QUICKLY PACKED her few things, then went to the study and sifted through the odd scraps Michael had retrieved from the lightwell, finding nothing noteworthy. Still, she left the bag by the door and would take it with her when the time came for her to vacate the apartment.

With still a few minutes before Michael was due, she picked up *Goddess Sites: Europe* and turned to the section on Spain with the vague idea that the date of Cristiana's death coincided with . . . and there it was!

Saint Agatha's Day. That's what had struck her about the date Carlos Ballester mentioned when they'd talked in his study. February 5, the day women take over and men's activities are restricted to domestic chores.

How odd, she thought, that Cristiana would be killed that particular day, when, very likely, the chore would have fallen to a woman.

. . .

Weatherwise, it was an unpredictable day. As if the gods were calling a square dance, heavy squalls do-si-doed with piercing sunlight.

Queenie waited just inside the apartment building's entrance. When Michael pulled up out front, she darted outside and hopped in the car.

"Michael, when we first met and were stuck in the elevator you said Carlos Ballester was the richest man in Catalunya, then you amended that," she said while fastening her seat belt. Michael shot up the slick, narrow street, passing Freddie's Jag. A quick glance reassured Queenie that the expensive car had survived a night on the street.

"Right. Well, last year, after graduation, I got a management job at one of his factories outside Barcelona. My position gave me access to his financial records. . . . I wasn't impressed—in fact, I was shocked. He'd suffered some severe losses that year, when two of his factories burned down. Interestingly, he'd just gotten married, and it wasn't hard to figure out where a large chunk of profits were going—money that logically should have gone into rebuilding. Then, too, he was spending more time in Rome on Vatican business.

"Frankly, I was surprised to learn he was responsible for financing Señor Frazier's movie. If it doesn't make any money, Don Carlos will probably be in serious trouble."

Without comment, Queenie assimilated this information, wondering if any connection existed between Patterson's murder and Ballester's weakened financial situation.

Around eleven, Michael dropped her outside the British Institute on Calle Amigo, then drove off to find a parking space. Queenie dashed up the steps and through glass doors. Straight ahead were stairs leading to classrooms. To the right, a uniformed, unarmed guard stood outside another set of glass doors, through which she could see the library. In English, the guard inquired after her business. She told him she wanted to see about getting a library card. Graciously, he held the door for her.

Queenie approached a woman in a crisp white blouse working behind a high counter just to the left of the door. Beyond were rows of tall, free-standing shelves with reading areas provided in the single long room. Nearby, a man sat reading a newspaper; the whispery sound of the turning pages offered the only noise in the otherwise quiet room.

"I'm wondering if you can help me," Queenie began while reaching in her satchel for her wallet. "My name's Queenie Davilov."

"Yes?"

Queenie flashed her private investigator's license and lowered her voice. "Do you know a British writer by the name of Digby Patterson?"

A moment of heavy silence passed, but Queenie felt reassured by the woman's stunned expression.

"It's very likely he patronized this library," Queenie prompted.

The woman licked her lips. "Excuse me a moment, please."

Queenie moved aside as a man dumped a pile of books on the counter; her sapphire eyes studied the librarian's steadily reddening face and long neck. The woman glanced nervously at Queenie, obviously uncomfortable with being scrutinized. Politely, Queenie shifted her attention to the chosen authors: Evelyn Waugh, Anthony Burgess, Trollope, and Hardy. The guy was either an optimist or a speed reader.

As the man moved away with his load, the librarian

stepped down from behind the counter and began pushing a trolley laden with books to be reshelved. She wore a navy blue skirt and sensible shoes.

"Digby Patterson," Queenie persisted, following the woman between two towering shelves.

The woman inserted a volume on a high shelf. Queenie noticed the dampness under the sleeve of the white blouse.

"Please, if you knew him—"

"Yes, I knew him!" she hissed. Then she took a deep breath, her eyes never meeting Queenie's.

"Are you aware of what happened to him?"

"Of course. I read the newspapers. Look, I can't talk here."

"How about meeting somewhere for coffee?"

The woman shelved a couple more books before she spoke. "We close from one to four. There's a wine bar across the street. I'll meet you there at quarter past one." Then she quickly moved away, seemingly absorbed in restocking chores.

Queenie gave the guard a quick smile on the way out. She didn't feel like waiting for Michael in the lobby under the man's watchful eye, and stepped outside just as the rain began to fall. Across the street she spied the wine bar the librarian had mentioned, then noticed Michael heading up the street while opening a black umbrella. She hurried down the steps.

The rain pounded the fragile-looking fabric while they huddled together. She told him about her upcoming meeting with the librarian. "In the meantime, I'll check out the North American Institute," she said. "But I'd like you to stay here and keep eye on her. If she bolts, follow her." Then Queenie quickly described the woman.

He regarded her skeptically.

"Most likely she'll stay put. She seemed to be working alone."

"I don't know about this, Queenie. I've never followed anyone. And the rest sounds boring."

She smiled slightly. "Most detective work is just that."

She spotted a cab and stepped out to hail it. While opening the back door, she called out, "Don't worry, Michael, you'll be fine."

The North American Institute was both larger and more modern inside than its British counterpart, though the library itself was smaller. She found it tucked away on a lower level.

A friendly, helpful woman in her mid-thirties, the American librarian, had only just heard of Digby Patterson through the news, nor from newspaper photographs did she remember ever seeing him in the library. She was aware of the film but hadn't paid much attention to anyone working on it—with the exception of Tybalt St. Germain. She suggested Queenie try the British Institute, as it had a better selection of books on the Spanish civil war, and it was more likely that he'd done his research there.

Queenie thanked the woman and returned to the street to find a cab.

She entered the wine bar at about twelve thirty and took a seat by the window, where she had a good view of the British Institute. As she waited, sipping a cup of strong coffee, rain changed to hail, loud and hard like gravel falling from the sky. She thought of Oklahoma in spring—tornadoes, hailstorms, and sudden hot, humid days when the horses fretted. She wondered how her mother's tomato plants were doing. She thought of Chicken Little.

A few minutes before one, Michael loped across the street.

He plopped down in the empty chair opposite her own, his eyes glazed.

"She still there?"

"Oh yes. They've just closed for lunch. I almost wish she'd left. Those were the dullest two hours I've spent since school."

"Michael, why don't you get some lunch and take a table at the back. It's better if I talk to her alone."

Reluctantly, Michael left. About fifteen minutes later, Queenie watched the librarian slip across the street. The woman clutched in front of her a small leather handbag and a jacket that matched her skirt. Even at a distance, her worry and tension were unmistakable. Queenie felt the itch of excitement, wondering what sort of a tale this woman had to tell.

CHAPTER TWENTY-FOUR

WHILE INTRODUCING HERSELF, Anne Delaney slipped her jacket over the back of the chair.

"What can I get you?" Queenie asked, rising.

"Vol Damm, if you don't mind."

"Anything to eat?"

"Thank you, no."

Queenie considered Anne's choice of beverage to be a good sign. The stuff was potent as hell.

Queenie set the glass and bottle in front of Anne then slid into her seat.

"I'd like to see your passport, please," Anne said coolly.

Being accustomed to presenting her identification, Queenie handed over the document without flinching. Anne checked the photo, then flipped to the visas.

Viewed from close range, Anne belied the stereotype of someone who appeared slightly numbed from years spent in semi-quiet, someone who gradually began to look like a dusty old volume never checked out. She'd applied fresh makeup before coming over, and a fruity perfume. Queenie reckoned her age to be moving upward from thirty-nine.

With a well-manicured, ringless left hand, Anne returned the passport, then raised her glass for a brief examination. Apparently satisfied, she filled it from the sweating bottle. "Frankly, I wanted to know how long you've been in Spain," she said.

"And whether or not I'd been here at the time of Digby Patterson's death."

"So tell me why an American detective is asking after him?"

"I was hired to do so," she answered truthfully but evasively.

"That doesn't tell me anything. Who hired you?"

"And that's confidential. Consider me an objective observer gathering information—like you did for him."

Her gray eyes began to shine in a silvery way. "You're right, I did help him with his research. We, uh—" She stopped abruptly and drained her glass, then quickly refilled it.

"You were lovers?"

The silvery shine, Queenie now realized, came from slight tearing. Anne took a moment to compose herself. Then she regarded Queenie squarely. "I suppose a young woman like you finds it hard to believe someone in the movie business would be interested in an unglamorous librarian."

"Not at all," Queenie said, then added quickly, "besides you're very attractive. When did you last see him?"

Anne seemed to relax a little. "A couple of weeks ago, just

before he went back to the parador for the last time. I'd found another book for him. He came to my flat to collect it. We had dinner and he stayed the night. He called that week to say that the film would be in hiatus for a few days while the director went to Cannes, and would I like to come up for the weekend. Said he desperately needed to talk someone *not* involved with the film."

Queenie remembered something, and got out the notebook where she'd jotted the telephone numbers Digby had entered into the parador's logbook. She showed them to Anne, who pointed out her own telephone number and the main number for the British Institute.

"Are you familiar with the other number?"

"Only the country and city codes for England and London. But, of course, that's where he made his home."

"Did you get the feeling he was in any danger or was being threatened?"

"He drank a lot, you see. On occasion he'd ring me after he'd been out with the lads. At those times it was difficult to tell what he was saying let alone his mood. Of course, I did manage to understand the love talk," she added sadly. "But it was all I wanted to hear."

Then she suddenly perked. "I say! Why don't I pop over to my office and ring this number in England? Wouldn't take but a minute, and you could order us some lunch."

Anne plucked a pen from her purse and jotted the number on the back of the small beer mat. Queenie noticed FOREVER embossed on the pen.

"I found a pen like that in the apartment where he stayed."

"Believe me, we didn't exchange them like love tokens.

It's a common brand." Then, leaving her jacket, she picked up her purse. "Won't be a moment," she said and left the bar.

Michael plopped down a moment later. "What am I supposed to do now?" he asked impatiently, clearly fed up with detective work.

"Look, Michael, I don't know how long this is going to take. If you've got something better to do, please go ahead and do it."

His expressive blue eyes screamed disappointment. She felt a little guilty for using him. "How about I treat you to dinner?"

"You'll be okay for now?" he asked.

"Wherever I go, I can catch a cab."

"All right then."

She smiled nervously, anxious for him to leave before Anne returned. "Why don't we meet outside the apartment around seven." Then she thought of something to keep his interest piqued. "One thing you can do is read the papers. Catch up on the latest developments for me."

"Okay. But unless you just want tapas, let's make it nine. It's common to dine late in Spain, even ten."

"Fine. Nine it is."

He seemed glad now to be of use again. Before leaving he came around the table and kissed her full on the mouth. Then he touched her cheek and left.

"Holy Mother, Davilov," she muttered, hoping his apparent affection wouldn't complicate matters even further.

Queenie ordered a couple of ham rolls and two more Vol Damms. By the time she finished her sandwich, Anne still hadn't returned. Queenie drank her beer and smoked a couple of cigarettes. Then she drank Anne's beer, wondering if the woman had been cornered on library business.

To prove her own optimism, she ordered another beer for Anne and a coffee for herself, and watched the rain come and go like a silvery curtain suddenly dropping then dissolving into sunlight. Surely Anne would return. After all, she'd left her jacket.

At two thirty, while Queenie considered calling Joey collect from the bar, Anne scurried across the street, holding a notebook on her head for protection from the rain.

Her face flushed with youthful excitement, Anne shook the raindrops from the notebook and, between bites of the sandwich, related what she'd discovered.

"Sorry it took so long," she said after swallowing a mouthful. "That number's for a publisher in London. I must have been routed through the entire company before finding the proper person, a children's book editor. Rather difficult since I had no clue why Digs had rung them in the first place."

After finishing her sandwich, she seemed to settle down. "Jolly good, you're a smoker," Anne said, noticing the butts in the ashtray. "Unless you had a visitor."

"They're mine. Go ahead."

Anne offered Queenie a Ducado, a Spanish brand. Queenie accepted and then lit Anne's and her own. "Anyway, Digs had rung them to inquire about the author of the last book I gave him. It's rather an obscure children's book I'd come across. I went back into the library and found that Digs hadn't returned it. And we have no other copy."

"What's the title?"

"*Child of the Time.*"

The paper Queenie had found in the pamphlet immediately came to mind; she figured that Patterson had made note of it while on the telephone. Something else: Queenie remembered the fanged boy on the cover of a book she'd seen while looking through the small library in the parador's tea room, and mentioned it to Anne.

"Maybe you could check to see if it's ours. We certainly want it back. The editor said it's been out of print for years."

"Do you remember what it was about?"

"Frankly no. Hadn't read it myself. When Digs started researching, we concentrated on nonfiction. He devoured everything. Later, he asked me to keep an eye out for anything at all, even fiction. One of the other librarians mentioned having seen something in the children's section, then brought the book to me. I believe I scanned the flyleaf and set it aside for Digs. Do you suppose it's important?"

"*Everything's* important."

Anne stubbed out her cigarette. "Well, as I said, Digs rang to find the author." Anne consulted a page in her notebook. "Someone named Carrasquer. The editor promised to ring him back, but with her work and whatnot, she forgot about it. Spent a good deal of our conversation apologizing, as she'd just heard what happened to him. But there it is. Until tragedy befalls us, we simply can't be bothered."

Queenie fell into a contemplative silence. A polite cough caused her to look up. Anne smiled slightly. "Sorry to interrupt, but I—"

The expression on Queenie's face must have stopped Anne midsentence. "What is it?"

Queenie didn't answer.

"I hardly know you," Anne said, "but there's something about you I trust. Is something wrong?"

Queenie debated with herself only briefly. "Anne. Both

your home and work numbers are on a log in the parador. Quite possibly they've simply been overlooked. That doesn't mean they'll continue to be."

Anne's youthful blush faded to white. Her body stiffened.

"Do you have any sick leave or vacation time coming?"

"Are you telling me I'm in danger?"

"Just to take precautions."

"I could lose my job."

"You could lose more than that," Queenie reminded her.

Anne suddenly coughed explosively. "Catarrh," she explained when she caught her breath.

"Perhaps a few days on a sunny beach would be beneficial," Queenie suggested pointedly.

CHAPTER TWENTY-FIVE

BEFORE A DISTURBED Anne Delaney left, Queenie jotted down the name of the British editor, Marilyn Markham. She took a cab back to the apartment.

It was a little after three, an hour earlier in England. While listening to the double rings, she willed Ms. Markham to be in. Indeed, the editor hadn't left for the day, but had stepped out of her office. Queenie left her name and number, adding that she would accept a collect call.

Queenie made a pot of coffee and waited a few more minutes. She calculated the time in L.A. to be between six thirty and seven A.M., but she didn't want to tie up the line with a call to Joey. The minutes moved with the speed of a jog through heavy mud.

Maybe once she spoke to Ms. Markham, she should vacate the apartment and find a hotel room, rather than wait to be asked to leave. But Michael would be arriving at nine.

For a few minutes her thoughts performed a dervish global dance, leaping erratically from Spain to England to California to Ireland. She wondered if Dick had left L.A., and what sort of hell Tybalt must be going through.

The phone rang, interrupting her thoughts. She grabbed it eagerly, only slightly disappointed that the caller was Joey.

As far as Joey could find, none of the principals involved in the film had any prior arrests, nor were they linked to Digby Patterson in any way that might suggest a motive for murder. "Patterson's got a closet full of ex-wives though. Maybe one of them did the deed."

"Given the circumstances, not likely. But thanks, Joey. I'll keep you posted, but I'm expecting a call and have to get off the line."

Impatience got the better of her and she called the London publisher. The receptionist said the editor was still out of her office and suggested that Queenie ring back first thing in the morning.

While dialing the number for the parador, she wished she'd called Ms. Markham from the bar.

Señora Pujol answered on the third ring. Queenie asked to speak to Freddie, but the señora said he was "bery drunk."

With a sigh of frustration, Queenie then asked the señora to check for the book *Child of the Time* in the tea room. But the señora was busy in the kitchen and anyway, the tea room was a mess and undergoing repairs.

Queenie hung up. Her skin felt sticky and gritty, and the moisture in the air exacerbated the sensation. You're overamped, Davilov, she told herself. Get cleaned up.

The shower refreshed her, though her level of tension

needed more than a pelting under a showerhead to alleviate. She laved her body and hair with the horse shampoo. As with any creative endeavor, an investigation had a cyclical life; the highs and lows were intensely focused. Time was an exponential factor favoring the perpetrator as more of it passed. In her experience she'd learned that there came a point, usually during a low, when one could either wait for something to happen or *make* something happen by following a hunch or taking a risk.

"If you want to catch a big fish, use live bait," her mother often said. She considering setting herself up. The best way would be to return to the parador, drop hints that she knew who'd killed Patterson, and wait for someone to come out of the woodwork ... and probably get herself whacked! Was sexual frustration making her stupid? Both Tybalt and Dick were dangerously heating her blood, and pheromones were influencing logic.

Closing her eyes, she lifted her chin, letting the water stream through her hair as she lightly shook her head. Foam floated down her body and into the tub. Maybe I should grab the first man I see, she thought offhandedly and opened her eyes.

Nat stood in the doorway.

Instantly, she reached behind and flipped the hot faucet to full, at the same time nudging the loose metal tubing. The showerhead reared back and shot Nathan with an unexpected blast of water. He jumped out of sight. Queenie leaped out of the tub, crossed the wet floor, then slammed the door and locked it.

"What the fuck do you think you're doing?" she yelled while turning off the water, her heart dancing in two-two-time.

"I heard the shower and thought someone, Andrew maybe, had snuck back in. No one's supposed to be here."

"Didn't you see Freddie's Jag on the street?"

"No!" he yelled back.

"What the hell are you doing here?" Then she remembered that the crew was no longer under house arrest at the parador.

"You have to leave."

Finding a dry spot by the bidet, she toweled herself. It wasn't as though this was unexpected. "Just let me get dressed and I'm outta here."

Dressing quickly, she left the bathroom. Nathan stood awkwardly in the foyer.

"You're disgusting," she snapped, her energy as disruptive as a tornado.

"I thought you'd gone back to the States."

"And how long did it take you to figure out that I hadn't?" She threw the keys at him just as the telephone rang.

Nathan started down the hall but she dashed past him and grabbed the telephone. He stood behind her.

"Hello?"

"This is Marilyn Markham in London. I'm returning a call from a Queenie Davilov."

"One moment please." With her hand over the mouthpiece she turned to Nathan. "This is personal, Nathan. Get out."

He gave her a sulky look, then went into the kitchen.

"Yes, this is Queenie Davilov." Lowering her voice, she said, "I'm interested in a children's book your firm published, *Child of the Time*."

"Yes, we've had several inquiries about the book lately. What is your interest?"

"Uh, I'm doing some research and would like to contact the author."

"Sorry, that's quite impossible. The author, you see, is dead. However, I've just been looking in the archives and came across some personal papers the author left with us."

"Would it be possible to see those papers?" Queenie asked, feeling a rising excitement.

"Actually," Markham replied, "the author left instructions for the papers to be made available to any interested parties."

"Great!"

"Would you like to come in, say, ten tomorrow morning?'

"In London?"

"That's where we are, Ms. Davilov."

"All right, I'll be there. But could we make it later?—I need to check on flights. How about noon and I'll take you to lunch?"

Marilyn Markham accepted the invitation, then said, "Oh, one more thing. Do you happen to read German?"

CHAPTER TWENTY-SIX

WHEN ANDREW HAD escorted her around the neighborhood, they'd passed a small hotel on Balmes, not far from the apartment. Now she registered there, and paid for one night. The desk clerk spoke English and gave her the information she needed about flights to London, then made a reservation for her.

Her room faced the noisy street, but she didn't complain. After such a busy day, she felt she'd sleep soundly. She telephoned Michael to inform him of her move, but there was no answer. Deciding a nap would recharge her now emotionally exhausted batteries, she phoned the desk for a wake-up call at eight thirty, then dozed off.

At eight forty-five she hurried through the rain to a milk bar directly across the street from the apartment house. She ordered a cola and sat by the window to watch for Michael.

A few cars and cabs passed by, but there wasn't much activity on the street. She saw a man in a dark trench coat carrying an umbrella leave the building next door to the one in which she'd stayed. He glanced down the street, as if to see if a cab was coming. A car passed, illuminating him momentarily. Queenie started. It was Señor Pujol; his bulb-shaped head was unmistakable. What was he doing in the neighborhood? she wondered.

She checked the time. It was a few minutes past nine. When she looked up, he'd gone. Maybe he'd driven Nat into town. But why had he come from the adjacent building? Visiting friends or relatives?

In the distance she heard sirens, a sound reminiscent of World War II movies. She thought of Digby Patterson, and wondered what his interest had been in the author of *Child of the Time*. Whatever mattered to Patterson while he was here required a follow-up.

The sirens grew more and more shrill, drawing the proprietor of the milk bar from behind the counter. He stepped out on the wet sidewalk. A moment later, several police cars converged in front of the apartment house, blocking the street.

What's going on? Queenie thought, becoming alarmed. She saw a blue-jacketed *portero* scurry out of the building from which Señor Pujol had emerged. The portero ran to the building and unlocked the front door. Several policemen dashed inside.

Queenie got up and joined the proprietor under the awning.

"*Qué pasa?*" she asked.

He shrugged. "*No lo se.*" I don't know.

Horns set up a raucous chorus as more people began to appear, some leaning over balconies, others jumping out of their blocked vehicles.

She felt someone brush her sleeve and turned to see Andrew Coachman holding a glass of wine.

"A bit of excitement," he commented, his face flushed. "So, you're still here. Terrible about Digs, isn't it?" He lurched slightly. He seemed to treat the situation as a dull cocktail party momentarily invigorated by the arrival of uninvited guests. "Rather a good thing I lost the job. Writers being treated shabbily is one thing, but to murder—"

Suddenly, someone grabbed her arm. She jerked around and saw Michael. His expression was apprehensive. He spoke in a low, urgent voice. "Come with me."

"Nothing like a spot of romance," Andrew said and raised his glass. "A bit of the old in-and-out?"

She barely glimpsed Andrew's lecherous grin before Michael rushed her down the street.

"Michael! What's going on?"

The line of cars was building; the noise was painful as drivers sat on their horns. Even if Michael had answered, she probably couldn't have heard him. In a determined silence, he led her down the hill, across a broad avenue—General Mitre—and finally stopped outside the entrance to the Padua metro station.

Drizzle turned to rain. Michael stepped into the street to hail a cab. After a few moments, one slid to a stop beside him. Michael jumped inside. Queenie followed.

In Spanish he gave the driver an address. As the cab darted into traffic, Michael bent over and shook the water from his hair.

"What was going on back there?" Queenie asked, gripping her satchel.

"We'll talk when we get to the restaurant," he replied grimly.

After a fifteen-minute ride, the cab stopped on a quiet street in Sarria in front of a small restaurant. "I'll see to the fare," he said. Queenie got out, sheltering from the rain in a tiny alcove. The *tick tick* of the idling cab brought to mind a bomb, and seemed to underscore the explosive nature of her experiences in Spain.

Taking her arm, Michael led her inside. A plump blond woman who looked to be in her forties greeted Michael like an old friend, then guided them down the narrow passage between booths and the bar to the table at the back. None of the booths, and only a couple of the bar stools, were occupied.

A bottle of red wine and two glasses appeared before they were even settled. Michael poured and the blond woman returned with two towels.

"You ready to tell me what's going on?"

"Maybe we should eat first. Don't want to spoil your appetite."

"Don't be ridiculous."

"Yes, I doubt anything would spoil yours."

He looked at her for a long moment. She crazily wondered if he'd somehow heard that just the other day she'd dug up a dead body. He licked his lips, then swallowed loudly.

"Let's order," he said and motioned to the blond woman.

"Fine. I'll have whatever you're having."

The woman rattled off a menu in French. Michael ordered quenelles and endive salad for two. The blonde smiled her approval, then disappeared down a set of circular stairs across from the table.

"Kitchen's in the basement," Michael said while twisting the stem of his glass. He stared into the wine. "While I was in school I dined here almost every night."

"Michael!"

He suddenly looked up. "There's a body on the tennis courts!" he blurted.

"The tennis courts below the apartment?" she said breathlessly, the hairs on her arm rising.

"The description fits Nathan. . . . Queenie, did you—" He seemed unable to finish the question.

She frowned, then the implication hit her. "Holy Mother! You think I pushed him off the balcony?" She jerked back against the booth.

"You were there . . . weren't you?"

She told him about Nathan barging in while she was showering, and that she'd checked into a hotel on Balmes and later waited for him at the milk bar. For the moment, she kept Señor Pujol's appearance to herself, primarily because she wanted to hear Michael's story.

Relief flooded his face. He grabbed her hand and squeezed it, then explained. He'd been driving around looking for a parking place, and had finally found one just up from the tennis club when the police cars, then an ambulance, arrived. He'd hung around to find out what was happening.

"Someone said it was an American, that the police got the ID from a wallet on the body. Honestly, Queenie, at first I thought it was you. Then I heard it was a tall man with blond curly hair."

"And thought of me again," Queenie replied hotly.

"What was I supposed to think?"

"Under the circumstances, it's rather brave of you to keep our dinner date."

Their food arrived. While eating, Queenie considered possible scenarios, wondering which one the police would run with. Had he been pushed or did he jump? The latter seemed unlikely. Jerks like Nathan didn't kill themselves. Her prints were all over the apartment; Michael's too. Sooner or later the authorities would come looking for them.

But what about Señor Pujol? Though she'd seen him only for a moment, his oddly shaped head easily identified him. What had he been doing in the neighborhood, and especially around the time of Nathan's launch? And what possible motive could he have?

Her thoughts then turned to Andrew. He might have an additional set of keys—and she had witnessed him threatening Nathan. While he had appeared drunk on the street, that in itself didn't exclude him as a suspect. However, if he'd been in a bar at the established time of death, he'd have an alibi.

Then, of course, Michael also had a key. He could be lying. Yet, there was something so guileless about Michael, he seemed far more capable of confession than deceit.

"Did you go through that bag of paper I collected this morning?" Michael asked.

"Damn! I left it by the door. But yes, I did. Didn't find anything of interest."

Michael mopped up the remaining sauce with a piece of bread, then pushed his empty plate to one side. "That tenant on the first floor is going to remember me," he said forlornly. "I might be a suspect."

She regarded him intently. "You're right."

"What should I do?"

"Wait till the news hits the press. At this point every-thing's hearsay. We don't *know* it's Nathan. And as improbable as it seems, if a note was left, chances are the police won't investigate."

"Do you think he killed himself?"

"*If* it's Nathan—no."

She glanced at her watch. Michael pulled out his wallet.

"My treat, Michael. I mean it."

Appearing embarrassed, he tossed some bills on the table, and waited outside while she paid the tab.

He was just getting in the backseat of a cab when she left the restaurant. Stooping down, she joined him. "Have the driver drop you off first."

While the driver sped through the rain-slick streets, she asked Michael if he'd found anything of interest in the newspapers. But he offered nothing she hadn't already heard from Freddie. Neither spoke again until the driver stopped near the tennis club.

Michael opened the door and stuck his leg out. "When will I see you again?"

"I'll call you."

"Why don't I believe you?" he said, then suddenly kissed her.

Gently, she pushed him away. "Go home, Michael. Get some sleep."

"You get a good night's sleep, too," he said wistfully and reached in his pocket.

"I'll take care of the cab, Michael."

Ignoring her, he gave the driver several peseta notes. Satisfied, the driver turned back around.

"Just one more thing," Michael said.

"What?"

"This feels like a Greek drama."

"How so?"

"You know, if you don't like the message, kill the messenger?" He stared at her for a minute. "Think about it. Nat was the messenger."

"Oh come on! You don't think I killed him because he told me to leave—"

Michael interrupted by suddenly exiting and slamming the door.

With a heavy sigh, she directed the driver to Carmella's bar just a few blocks away, then turned to watch Michael, shoulders hunched against the rain, as he unlocked his car.

She paid her part of the fare and hurried through the light rain to the Jaguar. She climbed behind the wheel and, after plotting the short trip with the map, set out for Prat de Llobregat airport. Indeed, she planned on getting a good night's sleep. Just not in Barcelona.

CHAPTER TWENTY-SEVEN

SHE PARKED THE Jaguar, believing the expensive auto would be safer in long-term airport parking than on the street. Inside the relatively quiet terminal, she canceled her morning reservation and boarded the last flight to London. She was unwilling to risk being detained in Barcelona. Possibly Michael would go to the police and, by relating his movements, bring her to their attention—and they might not allow her to leave Spain without permission, and in their own good time.

"Whoever killed Patterson," she mumbled to her reflection in the rain-stained window, "never expected his body to be found. Someone's perfect crime wasn't so perfect after all."

And what about Nathan Arturo? She'd felt distanced from the news of his apparent demise, but why not? She had no idea if Nathan's was indeed the body on the tennis court. For the sake of argument, however, if Nathan was dead, what linked him to Digs? Two murders were too much for coincidence. To take that a step further, wouldn't it prove Tybalt St. Germain's innocence? After all, Tybalt's current address limited his movements.

And how could Michael think she'd shoved Nat over the balcony? His reference to the messenger in Greek drama pretty well defined his thoughts. How absurd that, just because Nat had told her to leave the apartment, she'd kill him!

But at the moment, she had other considerations. Settling back in her seat, she said a prayer to the Goddess and took the Jim Rice baseball card out of her wallet for travel duty.

The aircraft thundered down the runway, the passengers lightly bouncing in their seats. Queenie closed her eyes, and a host of impressions, angelic and demonic, real and imagined, suddenly bubbled up in a frothy surrealistic soup that would have made Catalan native sons Dalí and Gaudí proud. Certainly not images for the fainthearted.

Since she had been in London once before to attend her twin brother's wedding, the city wasn't altogether unfamiliar to Queenie. She and another passenger from her flight shared a cab from Gatwick into London's Victoria Station. From there, she caught another cab to the hotel near Green Park where she'd stayed six years ago. Fortunately, a room was available and, at nearly three A.M., her head hit the pillow and she fell fast asleep listening to *English* rain.

What had been a tight childhood relationship between Queenie and Raj soured after Rex's birth, when the twins were nine. Raj retreated into his multilingual world while Queenie looked after the baby.

Rajah Davilov's gift for languages appeared early and attracted the attention of the language department at the University of Oklahoma, where he was tested at age eleven and enrolled in Spanish and French summer school courses. At age twelve, he was allowed to audit university classes in Greek and German. At fourteen he was sent to a private school in Washington, D.C., with tuition and board paid for by a local oilman for whom Raj later translated complex foreign documents without charge.

After graduation from the American University in Washington, D.C., he went to work for Sir Wycombe Summerville, a close associate of the oilman who'd been his early benefactor. Raj declined offers from the State Department, the Central Intelligence Agency, and the World Bank, among others.

At age twenty-six, he married Tasmin Summerville, the boss's only child, entrenching himself in the enormously wealthy family. Queenie had been the lone family representative at their London wedding—the only Davilov to receive an invitation and a round-trip ticket. Queenie had seen neither Raj nor Tasmin since their wedding day; she wondered how or if either had changed.

Just after the nine-o'clock wake-up call, Queenie telephoned Raj, not really expecting him to be home, but then again, not really knowing what to expect.

"The Davilov-Summerville residence," a subdued male voice answered.

"Raj, please."

"May I ask who's calling?"

"Certainly. His former wombmate."

There was a pause, then, "One moment, please."

Several minutes ticked away. She wondered if some servant was wandering through miles of a castle's corridors searching for the lord.

"Ha! Q! I don't believe it."

Somewhat startled when he finally came on the line, Queenie said excitedly, "Raj. It's great to hear your voice."

"What's this? Need money? You could have reversed the charges."

"Don't be an ass. I'm in London."

"My God. Whatever for—and why didn't you tell me ahead of time?"

"There was no ahead of time. I've got some business here and thought I'd try and see you if you were in town."

"Well, I've got some business to deal with, but I'll be free in a few hours. How about lunch?"

"I'm meeting someone at noon. Why don't I call when I'm finished?'

"Don't be silly! Just come on over. You've got the address? I'll see you then."

Promptly at twelve noon, Queenie presented herself to the receptionist at Armdale Publishers, Ltd. Told to take a seat, she waited for Marilyn Markham to come down.

In a few minutes, a stunning, vivacious redhead in her early thirties entered, filling the small reception area with fragrance and energy. Expecting a grandmotherly type to edit children's literature, Queenie thought this woman seemed more a candidate for best-sellers written by authors like Barbara Taylor Bradford. She wondered if all editors dressed so stylishly, and contrasted her own writing uniform—cut-off sweatpants and frayed T-shirts weightless as foam—to Marilyn's pale-green wool suit and yellow silk blouse accented by substantial gold jewelry.

In the crowded but subdued daub-and-wattle pub where they lunched on shepherd's pie and mugs of hot tea, the two women drew some attention. Queenie thought they looked like a gallery owner and a struggling artist—or maybe a social worker and her client.

Queenie explained she had heard *Child of the Time* might be of use in research she was doing on the Spanish civil war.

"Why did you ask if I read German?"

Marilyn swallowed a mouthful of meat and potatoes before answering. "Most of the correspondence is written in German. However, there are some letters in English that the original editor saved."

"Is the original editor available?"

"Been dead for years."

"Have you read the book?"

"Umm, no I haven't. After speaking to a woman from the British Institute in Barcelona yesterday, I decided to check the archives. Interestingly, the author sent a packet before her death with instructions to make the enclosed materials available to researchers. It's not unusual, but a bit odd, considering the book is merely children's fiction."

"Where did the author live?"

"A place called Arenys de Mar in Spain. I'm not familiar with it." Neither was Queenie.

"When did the author die and when was the book published?"

"The book was published in nineteen fifty-five. She died ten years later."

"She write any other books?"

"*Child of the Time* was the only book of hers we published. Of course, she may have done other work under another name for another publisher."

Back at Armdale, Marilyn settled Queenie in an empty conference room and brought a packet comprised of two files, one containing the correspondence between "H" and "M" written in German, the other holding three letters written directly to the publisher in English. The letters from "H" were typewritten carbon copies. Those from "M" were in a spidery longhand. Unable to read German, Queenie ascertained only dates: a few letters written from 1945 to 1950, considerably more between 1951 and 1954. The last letter was from "H" and was dated a few days before Christmas 1955.

Queenie quickly read the letters in the second folder, all harsh criticisms of the book. The letter writer lived in Surrey, and, Queenie was somewhat astonished to note, her name was Mary Frazier. Could she be the same woman who'd been Freddie's governess?

While an assistant made copies of the two files, Queenie and Marilyn chatted for a moment in the editor's cramped office.

"Would you have the author's full name?" Queenie asked.

Marilyn frowned. "Hmm." She mumbled something, then excused herself and left the office. The assistant returned with the freshly made copies and set the original packet on Marilyn's desk.

Queenie waited another thirty minutes. When Marilyn reappeared carrying some papers, she apologized for taking so long and handed Queenie a copy of the book. "Hannah Schlecht Carrasquer," she said.

Holy Mother! Queenie thought excitedly.

"Since I can't let you have the book, I made a photocopy. You'll find all the pertinent information for your bibliography. Do let me know how your project turns out."

"Absolutely. I have a feeling I just might be close to finishing."

CHAPTER TWENTY-EIGHT

A BUTLER ANSWERED the door. Laughter rumbled from somewhere within the three-story town house.

"Hi. I'm Raj's sister, Queenie."

Not a twitch of surprise registered on his granite face. "He's expecting me."

The butler showed her to a small room off the foyer, a sort of waiting room. There were several comfortable chairs and a coffee table on which magazines in assorted languages were neatly arranged.

"Wait here, please," the butler said and left.

She went to the window and looked out at the tidy patch of lawn contained within the black wrought-iron fence, and beyond it, the street, shiny as patent leather. This was their most modest abode. They also had access to an estate in

Devon, where Sir Wycombe spent most of his time, another in Scotland, and holiday homes in the south of France and on the Gold Coast of Australia near Brisbane.

Queenie sighed, feeling a twinge of envy. Raj had traveled about as far as he could from the earthy, gritty ranch in Oklahoma—whereas she'd only exchanged red dust for exhaust fumes. She wondered if his illegitimacy had ever presented any problems with the Summervilles. Probably not; Raj's genius had the power to overshadow any family blemishes. On the other hand, two of those blemishes, L.J. and Rex, hadn't been invited to the courtly wedding. But then, L.J. would probably have laughed raucously to see her oldest son in gray morning dress and top hat.

"Hi, Q," he said lightly, as if only a few hours instead of years separated them from their last physical contact.

Queenie jerked around. For a moment, neither spoke.

They were as fundamentally identical as male and female twins could be. His hair was black and thick as her own, and, maybe as a slight protest to convention, he still wore it long, pulled back in a pony tail. He wore a cable-knit sweater, faded jeans, and moccasins.

The thought suddenly struck her that this is how she'd look with a mustache. She suppressed the urge to laugh.

They hugged each other tightly.

"What's so funny?" he asked, his hand going immediately to his mustache, as if he had read her mind. "Taz calls it her little caterpillar."

"You look distinguished."

"Feels like someone left their coat under my nose. So, how long are you here?"

"I'm heading out in a couple hours."

"Well let's have a drink and you can fill me in on what you're up to. Taz's having some friends over for lunch. We can talk in my sanctorum."

"Maybe you can help me with something."

They entered an adjoining room in which the furniture was worn and without distinction. A hodgepodge of books filled the shelves along three walls: leatherbound reference dictionaries sharing space with hardbacks and paperbacks in numerous languages.

He turned on a floor lamp between two forest-green leather chairs positioned in front of a cold fireplace, and watched her as she surveyed the room. In the shadows behind them, she saw an ordinary desk, and an upright piano covered with sheet music.

"I've taken up piano," he said, and added self-deprecatingly, "which is why my study is located more or less out of the way."

Queenie sat down in one of the leather chairs, recalling her own which had been lost when the apartment house was condemned.

"Talked to L.J. lately?" he asked.

"Not directly. I called the ranch to tell her about my trip. She wasn't around so I talked to Bobby," she said, referring to the ranch foreman. "She's quit drinking, you know."

"In which case, there's a helluva lot more whiskey in the world for the rest of us." He opened a cabinet built next to the fireplace, housing a wide selection of liquor, glasses, and a small refrigerator.

"What'll you have?"

"Whatever you're having."

While he filled two highball glasses with ice, he said, "And baby brother?"

222

"Read the sports section of any American newspaper," she replied testily. Raj didn't share her pride in their younger sibling's prowess on the baseball diamond. Raj's attitude not only mystified but angered her.

"He's got a nickname," she went on. " 'The Sequel.' "

"The sequel to what?"

"Babe Ruth."

He handed her a glass with two fingers of something amber, his eyes sharp and hard as obsidian arrowheads. "All I can say is, he certainly benefited from having you as mother, father, coach, tutor, ad infinitum."

"He is your brother," she said. She waited for a moment but he didn't comment. She sipped her drink. There was a little too much sharp on his knife; time for a change of subject. "Wow! Great stuff!"

"Twenty-four-year-old scotch. As anglicized as I've become, I still prefer whiskey with ice—though my mother-in-law considers the practice on a par with farting in a royal reception line." He rattled the ice in his glass and smiled.

"And have you done that?"

"Not yet. But then I've not been invited to any royal receptions."

She laughed, then synopsized her latest adventures, concluding with the recent trip to Armdale publishers.

"Maybe I can help. Let me see those letters."

"Great. But if you're busy, there's someone in Barcelona I can ask," she said, thinking of Michael.

"Don't be silly. I'd love to do it."

She'd planned to ask him, but felt better that he had offered first. Now she could quickly learn if the letters had any bearing on the script. But she felt strongly that they did, believing Hannah Schlecht Carrasquer to be none other than

Cristiana's former personal maid. Hopefully, she'd also find out Mary Frazier's role in this drama.

"Can I afford you?" she said lightly, though while reaching into her satchel she noticed her hands were trembling. Forcing herself to calm down, she passed him the photocopies.

"Probably not. But I'll make an exception."

She handed over the documents. "While you're doing that, do you mind if I use your phone? I'll leave you money for the call."

"Help yourself, Q," he said, and nodded to a telephone on the desk. "And don't worry about the charges."

He went to a bookshelf and pulled out a German dictionary, took paper, pen, and a small tape-recorder from the desk, then settled into one of the green leather armchairs.

"Now leave me alone," he instructed.

Appearing absorbed in the work, Raj didn't seem to notice she was even in the room as she called the parador.

"*Dígame!*" Señora Pujol answered.

Queenie identified herself, then asked to speak with Freddie, hoping the producer hadn't turned a day's drinking into a binge.

"He shooting movie with Isobel."

Something major must have happened to put the film back into production. "Is there someone else I could talk to?"

"*Momento,*" Señora Pujol said. Queenie heard the phone being put down, then voices in the background. A man came on the line. It took a moment for her to recognize the speaker, since she'd hardly expected *him* to come on the line.

"Tybalt?" Her heartbeat shot up. "What's going on?"

"The show. At the moment, anyway." He sounded tired.

"Are you all right?"

"Quite. Our delightful innkeeper has allowed me the use of her kitchen. Where are you? Freddie's been calling all over trying to find you."

"I'll be there later," she replied evasively.

"In time for dinner?"

"Not sure."

"Well, I certainly look forward to seeing you, Queenie," he said huskily.

She hung up, not comfortable with asking questions that implied she wasn't on top of developments. Well, she wasn't, but she didn't want Freddie—or even Tybalt—to know that. Maybe she could find answers in the British newspapers.

There was a single knock, then Tasmin's red-gold head poked into the room. "Raj, whatever are you—" She caught sight of Queenie and stepped into the room.

Queenie saw the odd speculative look in Tasmin's eye, the same one she'd noted when they first met. Given her close resemblance to Raj, Queenie wondered if Tasmin felt physically attracted to her.

Tasmin had gained weight since the wedding, but the same seemingly poreless, cream-colored skin carpeted her now more abundant flesh.

"Well. What a surprise."

"I just happened to be in town."

"Will you be staying for dinner?"

Queenie smiled and shook her head, not quite knowing if she'd just been invited or told that she would be tolerated at the table. "But thank you," Queenie added in either case.

"Fine," Tasmin said then turned to Raj, who had yet to acknowledge his wife. "Raj," she said insistently. When he didn't look up, she said, "Honestly," and strode to his side,

2 2 5

where she stood like a pillar of the finest marble. Raj looked annoyed, but stopped dictating into the machine.

Queenie returned to the green leather armchair. The couple spoke for a moment in hushed tones, then Tasmin moved over to Queenie and lightly held Queenie's arms while air-kissing each cheek. "Delighted to see you, but I must get back to my friends," Tasmin said, her sincerity impossible to ascertain.

A vision of the three of them naked in bed appeared in Queenie's mind. She bit her lip.

"I amuse you?" Tasmin abruptly pulled back.

"Funny, that's what I said when I saw Queenie," Raj quipped without looking up from a notepad.

Queenie flushed. "I'm sorry. It's just that, well, I'm a little tense."

"Whatever for?"

"Nothing really."

"Queenie's been working on a film in Spain, darling."

"It wouldn't be the one where the writer was murdered?"

"Hopefully, that's the *only* one. But yes."

"How absolutely fascinating. Oh I do wish you could stay! Did you know the American chap who killed him?"

CHAPTER TWENTY-NINE

SO TASMIN DAVILOV-SUMMERVILLE, the last person Queenie would have expected, dropped the latest bomb, the information gleaned from the British press. According to what Tasmin had read that morning, a suicide note had been found in the Barcelona apartment. Nathan Arturo had confessed to killing Digby Patterson out of jealousy of the writer's success.

Tasmin brought Queenie the papers, then went back to her friends. Queenie read that the residents in the apartment beneath the *sobre ático* had been on their balcony and witnessed Nathan's plunge and immediately called the police. Those questioned in the surrounding apartment buildings hadn't seen anything much. It had been raining and the penthouse apartment had been dark. With no interior lights on, Nathan hadn't been backlit when he took his leap.

Queenie wondered if someone not yet questioned might have a different story.

In about forty-five minutes, Raj concluded the translation, and fifteen minutes after that they were in the backseat of his black Bentley while Adam, the family chauffeur, drove them to Gatwick airport. The tape recorder and photocopies were in her satchel. She'd wanted to purchase a recorder to play back the tapes of Raj's translation during the flight, but he had insisted she take his.

During the drive, they tried to catch up on a combined twelve years of relative silence broken only by the exchange of Christmas cards. Outside the terminal she hugged her brother hard and lost some professional cool when a few tears escaped.

"Any nieces or nephews on my horizon?" she asked as, slightly embarrassed, she wiped her eyes.

"Tasmin's not into motherhood."

"Well, how about a couple of little bastards then?"

"You're wicked!"

They laughed, releasing tension in both of them.

"Listen, Raj, I appreciate your help and it's good seeing you."

"Sweet and certainly short. But why not come back when you're finished in Spain. Stay as long as you like. There's plenty of room . . . so much, we wouldn't even have to see each other."

Not exactly "I love you," but close enough.

The Avianca 737 touched down at Prat de Llobregat airport around ten P.M. Curiously, Queenie felt glad to be "home," though she doubted her welcome. What she carried in her satchel could ruin a reputation—and, to put it mildly, expose her to considerable hostility.

She picked up the Jag and drove to the hotel on Balmes to collect the few things she'd left in the room and to pay for the extra day. Back behind the wheel, she sat for a moment and rolled a couple of cigarettes for the trip north.

Child of the Time had been a quick read, and had left her enough time to listen to Raj's translation of the letters. Both the photocopied book and the letters pointed to a motive for Patterson's murder . . . probably Nathan Arturo's too. Michael had been right to equate Nat with the "messenger," though for the wrong reason. Nuria had mentioned seeing Nat enter the apartment late at night; Andrew had caught him going through the notes in the study. Unfortunately, Nat had discovered what Patterson, too, discovered, and had relayed the information to the interested party. And, Queenie surmised, that had been Nat's real job all along—to snoop.

She thought of Señor Pujol, and at the same time she recalled the narrow terrace off the bedroom on the street side of the apartment, where only about three feet separated it from the rooftop of the adjoining building. The police, she mused, should be questioning surrounding residents whose windows faced the street side as well as the tennis court side of the apartment.

She started the engine and pulled out into traffic, now accustomed to her right-side position and the wonderful driveability of the Jaguar. Maybe *too* wonderful, she thought. Her vehicles were leased and usually inexpensive Plymouths.

During the drive to the village she considered her options. The truth was one thing, saving her skin another. She now shared information that had put one man in a grave and sent another tumbling over a seventh-floor railing. In the States, her situation would be quite different. Here, though, she was an outsider and could not count on the support of the authorities. Hell, she thought, they probably wouldn't believe me. All she could do was present what she'd found—which was, after all, what she'd been hired to do.

For the remainder of the trip, her thoughts turned to the book's sad story, an odd choice for young readers. It was written from the viewpoint of a young boy trying to reconcile his older sibling's actions . . .

Can Jorge be my brother? I heard him talking to a man who sometimes comes to the house. The man gave him a wooden model of a German Junker that Jorge said I couldn't play with. I would never play with such a beastly toy! Jorge talked to the man about our mother. He told the man she has a lover and that she smuggles weapons to villages in the north. The man said Jorge was a very good lad and to keep watching mother . . .

. . . Jorge slapped me to the side when I tried to talk to the cacique, the political boss, to beg for mother's life. Jorge denounced our mother. At sunrise on the morrow she will be shot as a traitor when the real traitor is Jorge. He hates her because she does not love our father like Jorge thinks she should. I am only a small boy but now I hate because everyone hates. Am I merely a child of the time? How I wish father would come. But he is away on business. He is always away on business . . .

While the book was fiction and could be seen as an author's fantasy, the letters were another matter. They proved that

Child of the Time had been written with a specific purpose in mind: to illuminate Cristiana's betrayer.

Around midnight, Queenie pulled into the gravel lot. Fairy lights were strung along the veranda. Someone played a guitar while Nuria showed off her skills as a flamenco dancer. Carlos Ballester was her less lively partner.

Queenie parked the Jag near the equipment truck. Freddie suddenly appeared at the driver's side door before she'd jerked the keys from the ignition.

"Where in hell have you been?" he cried. Red wine sloshed from his glass, staining the gravel in the parking lot.

"Well, you wanted—"

"Never mind that! We wrapped the film a few hours ago. Been shooting since early morning, when Tybalt was released. Time for celebration!"

Holy Mother, she thought, feeling as if what she carried in her satchel was equivalent to the plague.

Tybalt suddenly appeared on her other side.

"She's mine, Freddie."

"Bloody swine. Thinks *he's* supposed to be the one that always gets the girl."

"I understand you shot the climbing scenes with Isobel today," Queenie said. "How was she?"

"Marvelous, bloody marvelous. She's been looking for you." Then he glanced around Queenie and up at Tybalt. "Beside herself, isn't she Tybalt? A lovely girl." Then he added absently, "Where has she gone off to?"

"Which room do I have now?" Queenie asked Freddie.

"Stay with me," Tybalt breathed in her right ear.

"Why, your old room, darling," Freddie said, gesturing expansively. "The police certainly don't need it anymore."

"And how thoughtful of Nathan to commit suicide." But

neither man seemed to have heard her. Apparently they'd all done an excellent job of forgetting that just yesterday Nathan Arturo had been alive.

Even Señora Pujol had joined the festivities; she was clapping in time to Nuria's rapidly clicking heels. Freddie and Tybalt steered Queenie to the drinks cart. Muncie slid up to the trio, smiling seductively at Tybalt.

"Freddie, we need to talk," Queenie said in a low voice, feeling like the only woman wearing hers at a delirious bra-burning rally. Freddie handed her a glass of Sangre de Toro. She accepted out of politeness and joined him in a glass-clicking toast to the film.

"Really. I'd like to talk *now*," she said.

"All right," he replied uneasily and grabbed a bottle of wine. "Let's go up to your room. Mine's a bloody mess."

They started inside the parador when Tybalt stopped her. "Going off with Freddie are you?"

"Believe me, romance is not on the menu."

His look softened. "Meet me for a drink then?"

"Sure. In a while."

Freddie darted behind the reception desk for a key and hurried up the stairs. She followed him to the room she'd previously tenanted. It had been cleaned and dusted, but, located over the veranda, was noisy.

Maybe like everyone else, she thought, I should get drunk and forget the rest. She sat Freddie down at the desk and pulled out the photocopies and the tape recorder while telling him of her meeting with Marilyn Markham, and what she'd learned at Armdale Publishers.

". . . And H. Carrasquer was none other than Cristiana's personal maid, Hannah Schlecht. Hannah wrote the book while living at a place called Arenys de Mar. Ever heard of it?"

"Why yes! It's on the coast a bit north of Barcelona."

"Now, I want you to listen to the tape. It's a translation of these letters. I think you'll find them"—she took a breath—"interesting." She tapped the photocopied pages of the book. "Read these, too. There's also a copy of the book in the tea room. I think Patterson left it."

She switched on the recorder and sat on the end of the bed to listen with Freddie.

The early letters presented a friendly exchange, but later, after 1951, when Hannah began writing the book, the tone changed considerably. "M" begged "H" not to publish the book, said that it would only resurrect the pain . . .

There came a loud, insistent knock on the door. Annoyed, Queenie answered, prepared to dismiss the caller. Freddie immediately shut off the tape recorder.

Isobel fidgeted outside the door, seemingly about to vacate her skin. "Please. Grandmother want see you," she halfwailed. Clutching Queenie's arm, she jerked her into the hall.

"Hold on, Isobel!" Queenie pulled free and reentered her room. "Freddie? I need to run into the village."

"Yes, yes. Run along. I'll . . . I'll just continue," he said weakly. His skin looked to be the color of wet ashes. Laughter invaded from beneath the balcony, contrasting with his now somber mood.

"Will you be all right?" she asked, his appearance drawing genuine concern.

"Of course," he snapped. "Just go!"

She closed the door. "Isobel? What's going on?" But Isobel ran down the corridor.

"Isobel!"

"*Muy tranquilo!*" But she certainly didn't act it, and ran down the stairs.

"How'd you know where to find me?" Queenie asked, hurrying to keep up.

"Señor Tybalt. He say to tell you not forget your date."

Instead of heading out the front, Isobel slipped out the back through the kitchen. This was not the way to the village. When they had passed the stand of plane trees, Isobel handed Queenie a flashlight, then darted into the darkness.

"Where are we going?"

"To grandmother. To sanctuary."

CHAPTER THIRTY

FOR THE NEXT twenty minutes, they wound through the trees, Isobel's hair shining in Queenie's light. The quarter moon hung above them, reminding Queenie of the Goddess's ancient bull horn crown. The deeper they went into the forest, the more primeval the environment felt. The sound of the revelers quickly faded, overpowered now by the night's edgy quiet.

Finally, after nearly losing her footing in some rough scree, Queenie followed Isobel into a cave. A feral scent assailed her. A narrow passage broadened into a wide chamber about six and a half feet high. She heard Isobel click off her light. She did the same, as she could see something black huddled behind several candles on the floor. Then the black thing lifted its head and Queenie saw a crone's face, her head covered by a black shawl. It was Isobel's grandmother.

Glancing around the chamber, Queenie's heart quickened

at the sight of spirals carved into the walls. She sensed that the abstract pictographs had been here for millennia—since long, long before William Morgan discovered that our own Milky Way was part of a spiral galaxy.

"Holy Mother," Queenie muttered.

"Grandmother talk to spirits," Isobel whispered. "They say, is time for truth. Grandmother say—*you!*"

"Me?"

Just then, the old woman rose and motioned to Isobel. "We go now. Have work. She follow."

"Where?"

"No talk."

Agile as a mountain goat, Isobel bounded fearlessly downhill, her long braid swinging like a pendulum. Queenie struggled to keep up, hoping the night wouldn't end with a broken bone or two. Finally, through the trees, she thought she saw the outline of building. Moving closer, she realized it was the facade of the church at the location.

What the hell are we doing here? she wondered. And found out soon enough.

Isobel entered the old cemetery. Suddenly alarmed, Queenie stopped. "I have to catch my breath," she said.

Flashing her light around, Isobel went ahead, passing between the crumbling grave markers. About ten yards ahead, Queenie saw the girl stop. She turned and waited for Queenie.

Wishing she had a bottle of her brother's wonderful Scotch, Queenie picked her way over to Isobel, who stood between two shovels.

"Isobel . . . you better tell me—"

Ignoring her, Isobel grabbed her by the wrist and pulled her over to a worn and cracked grave marker. Queenie stared at the pocked and broken granite. Nothing was carved into the surface. It was and always had been a blank slab.

"Here! Grandmother leave tools." And so saying, Isobel placed the flashlight on the ground. She picked up a shovel and began to dig.

What the hell have I done? Queenie thought. Set an example for gravedigging? She had never imagined that she would be engaging in such macabre activity *again*, but Queenie nonetheless followed her younger companion's example.

About thirty minutes into their labor, Queenie heard a sharp cackle and started. At the edge of the flashlight's arc, Isobel's grandmother squatted. She held out a bottle of wine. Licking her parched lips, Queenie took a break and drank from the bottle. Isobel didn't even look up.

The toothless old woman grabbed Queenie's hand and yanked her down. They sat together for a moment while the grandmother began speaking in a language Queenie had never heard. It wasn't even barely comprehensible Catalan.

Anyone coming upon the three women—one steadily shoveling dirt out of an old grave and two nearby holding hands—would have surely shrieked and run away.

"Grandmother *very* old," Isobel remarked cryptically without missing a beat in her rhythmic movements. "She say, like her, you have the sight but is most blocked. *Comprende?*"

Queenie sighed and started to rise. The grip on her hand became astonishingly viselike.

"Stay with grandmother."

"Isobel—"

"*Muy tranquilo, chica!*" Isobel admonished with a laugh. Meanwhile the grandmother continued her incomprehensible patter, then thrust the bottle of wine back at Queenie.

Willingly she drank, but was becoming increasingly uncomfortable just sitting while Isobel worked.

Finally, she simply jerked her hand away, breaking the connection. Whatever it was—something in the wine or in the old woman's energy—she felt refreshed as she picked up the shovel.

"Whose grave is this, Isobel?"

"Cristiana, grandmother say."

"Cristiana Ballester?" She stopped, the sweat on her body turning to ice.

"Sí. Grandmother say, truth in the grave. Is special."

Together they dug deeper. Conversation fell away, and together they set up a rhythm digging deep and steady. Thought vanished as the physical effort took over. Digging became a mindless, compulsive, mystical activity.

Finally, hitting something solid jerked Queenie's awareness back to the present. The top of a coffin.

With more eagerness than she thought herself capable of, Queenie pried the lid off. The old woman stood up and peered into the grave. Queenie stared at the bones, wondering if she was hallucinating.

Lying in the coffin was the skeleton of a wolf.

CHAPTER THIRTY-ONE

FREDDIE HAD MOVED up to the balcony and now sat with his back to the door, humming the Spanish ballads being sung by the still lively group on the veranda below. The wine bottle he'd brought to the room registered near empty and sat on the nightstand by the bed; beside it was another partially filled glass.

He jerked around at Queenie's entry and stared at her for a moment. "Good Christ you're filthy. Been digging up bodies again?"

"As a matter of fact, I have."

"You're joking!" he said in astonishment.

At that moment, the bathroom toilet flushed. Then Tybalt appeared, zipping up his trousers. Their eyes locked and Queenie felt a gelatinous substance take over her extremities. *Not now!* she warned herself, and abruptly turned back to Freddie.

"Freddie, there's something you need to see."

A fire crackled in the hearth and she became aware of a sharp, inorganic smell. She noticed the desk was empty but for the typewriter and tape recorder. All photocopies were gone.

She moved over to the hearth and peered at the fire. "You didn't!"

"Oh, but I did. Burned everything—including the tapes."

She sighed and sat heavily on the bed. "Why, Freddie?"

"Sorry old girl but—"

She glanced quickly at Tybalt and then meaningfully at Freddie.

"Would you leave us, old man?"

Tybalt looked at Queenie. "Will you be long?"

Freddie answered before she even opened her mouth. "Not at all. Our business is almost concluded."

Tybalt grabbed his wineglass off the nightstand and left. Freddie entered the room and pulled the chair over by the bed.

"Did Tybalt hear any of the tapes?"

"Of course not. Came up to see you. Joined me in a glass of wine. Only been here a few minutes."

Queenie took a deep breath. "I guess you realize that Maria was your mother."

He smiled weakly as tears welled in his eyes. "Dear God. For that alone, I can never repay you."

"Isobel's grandmother witnessed what was the execution and burial of a wolf." Queenie told him about what she and Isobel had just dug up.

His mouth dropped open in the classic expression of astonishment. "Good Christ!" he finally whispered.

"Anyway, Cristiana must have hidden in the mountains—

240

after all, she knew them well. I imagine she and Hannah communicated during those seven years you stayed with Don Miguel. Together, they arranged for her departure with you to England."

A silence broken only by the crackling fire fell for a few moments. Finally, Queenie asked, "Is Cristiana still alive?"

"She's very old but quite spry. I—" He paused to wipe his eyes. "I haven't seen her in years. Lives in a cottage not far from my grandparents' place. Christ! I never thought . . ."

Now to less emotional business, Queenie thought. "As you now know, you were right about her being betrayed. And that fact is what got both Patterson and Nathan killed."

He glanced up at her, his expression now remarkably steady. "Carlos."

"However, Carlos himself didn't commit the crimes. I think it was Señor Pujol. He's worked for Carlos for years, has access to both the parador and the Barcelona apartment, having been the *portero* at the building."

"How do you know that?"

"Señora Pujol told me the day I met Isobel."

"No, I mean, that Pujol did it?"

"I saw him outside the apartment building just after Nat's fatal fall. Why would he be there? As to Patterson's murder, there's not even circumstantial evidence to prove he did it, it just seems obvious to me. And Carlos isn't the sort of man to commit murder, but he is the sort of man to pay to have it done.

"Nat was his flunkie; he read what both Patterson and Andrew Coachman wrote, and reported back to Carlos. No doubt Carlos wanted to know what information was uncovered by the scriptwriters. Andrew really didn't have enough time to find out anything—but Patterson did.

"And, I don't believe Nat would have been killed if I hadn't found Patterson's body. Nat, you see, would know who had a powerful motive to want Patterson dead—Carlos, for whom he was spying. The ending Patterson was writing must have exposed Carlos as his mother's betrayer. Carlos could deny it as fiction, but the seed of doubt would be planted. There'd surely be a scandal. He could lose everything including, and maybe most importantly, access to the Vatican. Reputation and respect are everything to someone like Carlos. Finances aren't paramount. Hell, he poured money into this film when his businesses are suffering."

"How do you know that?"

"I have my sources. But you knew that, didn't you, Freddie?"

"You figured that out, too?"

"Hell, you bought the village fifteen years ago! Seems to me you were waiting for Carlos to show some weakness before you started the film. Also, if he declined to help finance the venture it would look suspicious. I mean, why wouldn't he want to be a part of a film that glorified his mother? Of course, there was some risk, but he thought he'd take care of that by bringing Nat on board. By making the film at a time when he was losing money, you just might have a shot at bankrupting him—payback for a lousy childhood—which makes me wonder about those acts of sabotage, *expensive* acts of sabotage."

She regarded him evenly. He drank down the rest of his wine and suddenly stood up. "I suppose we'll never know, will we?" He extended his hand. "Well done, Ms. Davilov."

Back to formality, she thought. "Are you going to the police?"

"The police? Of course not."

"But—"

"You were hired to probe and uncover—not to judge."

"Judge?" she said incredulously. "Two murders have been committed! This is about justice, not judgment. One of us has to talk to the police."

Instead of answering, he gave her a cryptic look, then walked to the door. "Would you mind waiting just a moment? There's something I need to do."

When he left, she poured the rest of the wine into her glass and walked out onto the balcony, which vibrated slightly from the loud rhythmic clapping just below. She heard the frenetic click of heels on concrete and figured that Nuria, or someone, still had enough energy to dance flamenco.

"*Olé!*" someone shouted.

Right, she thought ruefully. I could do with an *olé*.

Someone brushed her shoulder. She started and jerked around to find Tybalt standing beside her, the noise having cloaked his entry.

He gripped her arm and pulled her back into the room. "You ready?"

"For what?" She almost expected them to tumble back onto the bed.

"We're leaving."

"*Now?*"

"Don't ask questions. Just get your things together."

She picked up Raj's tape recorder and her satchel and joined him at the door. "Why—"

"Not a word!" he said, his expression a mix of apprehension and anger. Holding her hand, he led her quickly down the stairs, through the kitchen, and out the back door. Skirting the parador, they ran downhill into the village, now dead quiet and dark but for the headlights of the Jaguar.

243

Freddie stood by the idling automobile and flipped a cigarette away as they approached.

Tybalt slipped into the driver's seat and closed the door. With his hand on her arm, Freddie led a bewildered Queenie around to the passenger side. He opened the door and handed her an envelope.

"For your time," he said.

Woodenly, she sat down on the soft leather seat, still confused by the turn of events.

He leaned in and kissed her cheek. "Sorry, old girl. But it really won't do to keep you around. No, it won't do at all."

Then he slammed Queenie's door, and almost instantly Tybalt shot up the road and into the blackness that marked her last night in Spain.

CHAPTER THIRTY-TWO

"YOU'VE GOT UNTIL noon to get out of the country," Tybalt explained while he drove. He handed her a pack of cigarettes and asked her to light one for him and help herself. Then he continued. "After that, the authorities will be notified and you'll be detained for questioning about the assault on the parador." He paused and took a deep breath. "And the death of Nat."

"What? That's ridiculous!"

"Freddie thought I'd be the best person to convince you, seeing as how I've firsthand knowledge of Spanish jails."

"What else did he tell you?" she asked, trying to control her ire.

"Just that you'd gotten yourself in serious trouble. Frankly, I don't want to know any details."

"Holy Mother," she sputtered. "As if *I* was the criminal! The bastard!"

"Maybe you should open that envelope before it and you spontaneously combust."

She had momentarily forgotten the envelope. Now she quickly tore open the flap with her finger. She pulled out a check and two wads of money, one of five-thousand-peseta notes, the other of twenty-pound notes. In the dim interior light, she read a personal check from Freddie made out to her for four thousand pounds with a notation at the bottom, "For script doctoring."

For seven pages that will never appear on silver emulsion, she thought sadly, realizing too that the cash was a bribe, payment for silence. A stinking *little* bribe, given the potential for blackmail.

"He must have an awfully low opinion of me," she muttered.

"You're a screenwriter. You've got to accept that."

She only wished she could muster enough nausea to puke in Freddie's Jag . . . and aim the fountain at Tybalt's lap. Even he had lost his sex appeal.

"You have carte blanche to go wherever you want," Tybalt declared when they entered the airport terminal. "The cash is yours. I'm to put the ticket on my credit card. Freddie'll reimburse me."

"No thanks. I'll pay my own way." She didn't want anyone connected with the film to know her destination.

"Really, Freddie insisted—"

"Freddie can't insist. I don't work for him anymore." She stopped and extended her hand. "This is where we part. It's been nice meeting you, Tybalt."

"Look, whatever happened between you and Freddie has

nothing to do with me. I honestly would like to spend some time with you."

"Maybe someday," she said coolly.

"What about that garlic festival?"

She had to laugh and softened a bit.

"May I kiss you?"

"No. I have a ghastly taste in my mouth . . ."

Then she remembered something. She asked Tybalt to see that Isobel's grandmother got a set of false teeth. He agreed.

"Well then, as the Spanish say, 'Así es la vida.'"

She watched him leave. He looked back once and raised a hand in farewell. For a moment she thought about having refused a kiss from one of the sexiest men alive. Then, without regret, she went to buy a ticket to London.

Queenie stayed with Raj and Tasmin for several days, and saw very little of either of them. Raj was involved with some hefty translation, while Tasmin quickly lost interest in her sister-in-law when she refused to talk about the murder of Digby Patterson and his alleged killer, Nathan Arturo.

Queenie phoned Dick and talked to one of his housemates. Dick, she was told, had taken off for parts unknown. She called Eric, who was still partying in France, and left addresses and phone numbers where she could be reached over the next couple of weeks. She was thankful that he was still too preoccupied to ask for details of her latest job. Then she called Joey with an update (though not a very detailed one).

Sightseeing and pub-hopping eroded some of the sting of her dismissal from Spain—but not all. The day before departure, she called Marilyn Markham at Armdale Publishers.

Queenie mentioned having just learned that *Child of the Time* was linked to a film that had just finished shooting. Maybe Armdale would consider reissuing the book, as it would be a great tie-in with the film. Also, the letters left by the author would be super as an introduction. It was just a thought.

"When do you suppose the film will be released?" Marilyn asked, clearly interested.

"I'm not sure. My guess is, it'll be a contender at next year's Cannes festival."

Justice moves in mysterious ways . . . and sometimes needs a kick in the pants.

CHAPTER THIRTY-THREE

UPON ARRIVAL IN Cork, Ireland, Queenie rented a car and set out with a lightening heart. She stopped along the way for directions, and to buy a pair of Wellington boots and a wool cap. After a tranquil half-hour's drive she pulled up in front of an impressive stone manor house, parking beside several other cars. She slipped on the boots and cap, then, instead of presenting herself at the front door, went in search of the stables.

She passed a small crowd watching a boy of about fifteen put a sleek roan mare through her paces. No one seemed to notice her, but then, she looked like an ordinary horse person.

Inside the stable, she began checking each stall. Finally, in the last one on the left, she found him.

"Hi, cowboy."

A brush in his hand, Dick spun around. "Jesus Christ!"

"More like Mary Magdalene."

He kissed her over the stable door, then opened it for her. He tossed her a grooming brush and she slowly entered the stall, giving the magnificent raven-black stallion (the one with *four* legs) time to scent her. She extended her hand. He lifted his head, snorting and stomping, but quickly accepted her presence.

"Meet Teufel—it's German for 'devil.' "

Queenie took a position on Teufel's right flank and began brushing down the horse, who nickered contentedly. The scent of horse and hay relaxed her; she felt at home.

"I'm glad to see you," Dick said, looking at her over the animal's rump. "But let's not get Teufel excited."

"You don't seem too surprised to see me."

"A package arrived for you two days ago. I figured you'd show up."

"Who from?"

"Eric Diamond."

"What is it?"

"Q, I didn't open it. But it feels like a can of film."

Later, Dick called around and finally located a small theater that, for a fee, agreed to host a screening.

The can contained a reel of maybe ten minutes' worth of film. Queenie had no idea what it was; there was no note, nor a title marked on the can.

She and Dick sat in the otherwise empty theater. The lights dimmed. They could hear the projector tick as blank leader rolled on the screen.

Then, suddenly, her name appeared just below that of Digby Patterson: plain white letters on a black background. Her heart started to race.

The credit had been spliced to footage of the location in Spain. The camera, which appeared to have been handheld, moved slowly up a narrow street, stopping at a green door.

In the next cut, Queenie recognized the boy who'd played young Carlos. Some papers clutched in his hand, he knocked at the green door while looking furtively up and down the quiet street.

The door opened and he slipped inside.

In the next scene, young Carlos stood expectantly before a rough wooden desk on which was a candle. A man sat on the other side reading some slightly crumpled papers. He wore wire-rimmed glasses. After a moment, he put the papers down and regarded Carlos somberly.

"You would condemn your own mother?"

"I must do my duty. She is an enemy of Spain." (Queenie almost expected to hear his heels click together.)

"And has brought us guns to protect ourselves."

"A trick! She will tell the fascists you have weapons. They will come and destroy the village."

Light played across the man's spectacles and, for a moment, he looked like Himmler's twin. Slowly, he began to smile.

"Well done, lad. Your father will be proud."

The scene faded to black. The film was over. Lights in the theater came on and Dick looked at Queenie expectantly.

"What the hell was that?"

She didn't answer immediately, and, in fact, had been thinking about the time just before the police car exploded, when Freddie left her. Carlos had come out of the parador carrying a can of film.

What they'd just seen must be a print of footage Freddie

had shot at some time and stuck in the wardrobe in his room. Only two actors had been involved and, she figured, both were told to say nothing about the scene.

She realized now that her investigative work had given him sanction to use the scene in the film. When the film was released, Freddie would truly enjoy payback.

"Q?"

"I'll explain later. First I could use a drink." They collected the reel and left.

Outside the theater, with Dick's hand tucked in the waistband of her jeans, they strolled along the cobbled street toward the nearest pub.

Finally unable to contain herself, Queenie laughed. "Oh, Dick, I've just learned something marvelous."

"What's that, babe?"

"Revenge is best served up in public."